# THE COMING AUTUMN

LORI BUSMAN

Copyright © 2021 by Lori Busman

ALL RIGHTS RESERVED

Cover content is for illustrative purposes only. Any person depicted in the content is a model.

All rights reserved under the International and Pan-American Copyright Conventions. No part of this book may be reproduced or transmitted in any form or by any means, electronic or mechanical including photocopying, recording, or by any information storage and retrieval system, without permission in writing from the publisher, Lori Busman. No part of this book may be scanned, uploaded or distributed via the Internet or any other means, electronic or print, without premising from Lori Busman.

Warning: The unauthorized reproduction or distribution of this copyrighted work is illegal. Criminal copyright infringement, including infringement without monetary gain, is investigated by the FBI and is punishable by up to 5 years in federal prison and a fine of $250,000 ( http://www.fbi.gov/ipr/ ). Please purchase only authorized electronic or print editions and do not participate in or encourage the electronic piracy of copyrighted material. Your support of the author's rights and livelihood is appreciated.

This is a work of fiction. Names, characters, places, and incidents are either the product of the author's imagination or are used fictitiously, and any resemblance to any actual persons, living or dead, events, or locales is entirely coincidental.

COVER DESIGN: Lori Busman and Maria Vickers

FORMATTING: Maria Vickers

❋ Created with Vellum

# THE COMING AUTUMN

# DEDICATION

*Dedicated to my granddaughter, Haylee.
You are my sunshine, the light of my life.*

# PREFACE

This book is fiction. I tried to be accurate as far as dates and places of battles that took place during the Great War, however, any errors are completely mine. I wanted to portray characters based on actual people's diaries and letters written at the time of the war, and the events they experienced. I believe that the nurses in the first World War were among history's greatest heroes.

# PART I

# 1

## APRIL 1918

Sadie Prentiss settled down onto the small bench outside of the train station, her small suitcase at her feet. She looked down at it to make sure it was secure, then she leaned back and took a deep breath, willing herself to relax.

The crisp morning air carried just the hint of a breeze. She pushed back a wisp of curly, dark hair that had escaped the braid that she wore tightly wound around her head. Sighing, she tucked it back in and secured it with a pin. Her hair was constantly battling for its freedom, defying every attempt she made to confine it. When it was down, it hung nearly to her waist. Sadie had just arrived in France a few days prior. The three-week long voyage had been taxing, between the storms they had sailed through and the failure of her stomach to completely settle the entire time she was aboard. After a two-day rest at a boardinghouse near the port, she was now waiting to board the train that would take her most of the rest of the way to the field hospital near the front line. Eight hours on the train, then a couple by army truck or horse-pulled wagon.

After she had finished nursing school, Sadie had been asked to consider joining the war effort by using her considerable skills as a nurse and healer. At twenty-one years of age, she was young to be going overseas, but because she had unusual knowledge of plant medicine in addition to her very capable manner in the hospital, they had practically pleaded with her to go. Most of the nurses who went to the war front were older, plainer, and had dedicated their lives to nursing. Because she was small of stature as well as being young and pretty, she had been underestimated her whole life. She had gone to nursing school because she was good at caring for others and had learned so much about healing while she was growing up.

Sadie and her brother, Johnny, had been raised by their father after their mother had died giving birth to Sadie. Her father had been a gentle, hard-working man, but he had never recovered from losing his wife. Sadie did a lot of work around the family's small farm along with her brother but was also allowed to run wild a bit more than other girls.

Sadie smiled at the thought of how she had run through the meadows and woods near their home and how it had led her down the path to becoming a healer.

In the end of his life, she had taken care of her father, who had become ill and slowly weakened until he could no longer leave his bed. Her and Johnny never did find out exactly what was wrong with their father, but it was some sort of wasting disease; a cruel death that robbed the man of his ability to even walk and talk. The doctor couldn't do anything for him, so Sadie did everything she could to ease his discomfort with the knowledge she had of herbs.

She was seventeen when he died, and Johnny had been nineteen. They managed to keep the small farm going for two years, then, the United States joined the Great War.

---

From the time she had been around twelve years old, Sadie had a reputation around their small community in Southwestern Michigan as a healer of sorts. She had assisted with a childbirth when no one else was around as well as tended the neighbors' cuts, scrapes, belly troubles, sprains, and she had even set the broken arm of a young boy when he fell out of the hayloft at his family farm. She had done a fair job of it; when the doctor came, he said she had done well.

Sadie had learned about healing from a local healer named Hilda, who was a rather odd old woman who had long gray braids like an Indian, bright blue eyes and lived in a teepee part of the year, when the weather was good. The story was that Hilda had been lost in the wilderness out West when the wagon train her family was traveling with had stopped for the evening. She had been three years old. She had wandered away after supper, and when they discovered her missing, her family and the rest of the wagon train had searched for her for two days. As was common in those times when a child went missing, the train had to move on so it could get through the Rocky Mountains before winter. Hilda's devastated family was forced to move on without her.

She had been found in a meadow of wildflowers by an Arapahoe Indian woman who had been immediately taken with Hilda's beautiful blonde hair. Knowing that the girl was lost to her people, the woman had adopted Hilda into her own family. After discovering that her name was "Hee-da", as the little girl pronounced her name, the Indian woman, who was called Shining Dove, named her, "Hee-da

Nihooniienihi", which meant, "Hilda, Little Yellow Bird".

Hilda grew up with the Indian family, which was part of a small village in Western Nebraska. There was a missionary family that lived nearby, and they taught Hilda English as she grew up so that she would know how to communicate with white people when she was grown, when she might look for her birth family. Shining Dove and her husband, White Bear, also knew some English so they spoke both with Hilda as much as they could in Arapahoe and Hilda's native English.

Shining Dove was a medicine woman; a healer, and she taught Hilda everything she knew. Hilda learned from a young age all about which plant was used for which ailment. The Arapahoe were rarely sick. Hilda learned the value of each plant and helped her mother collect, dry, and store the plants they needed to keep everyone as healthy as possible. She also learned how to set bones and deliver babies. There were no barriers to keep her from learning everything there was to know. The Indians were much more forthright than white people; they simply did not have the notion that girls were of a more delicate nature and shouldn't be exposed to the dirty things in life. Hilda, or Yellow Bird as she was now known, became as well-versed in healing as Shining Dove. She grew into an adult, married, and had two children of her own, and she became famous for her blond hair and blue eyes and her reputation as a healer.

Hilda lived with the Indians for fifty years. When she was fifty-three years old, the white man's disease, smallpox, came and devastated the tribe. Sadly, Hilda's husband and daughter were among the victims. Nearly the entire village was wiped out by the horrible disease. Hilda, her son, Runs Fast, who had been married and lost his young wife in the outbreak, and a handful of others were all that was left of the once-thriving village. After they mourned their losses, Runs Fast and Hilda went further west, to Montana. They stayed with a cousin of Shining Dove, who had married a Cheyenne brave and went west. They lived there for five years, then Hilda decided to go to California to find her birth family. She had found out some years back from the missionary neighbor that she still had two sisters that were living. She had written to them and they were astonished that she was alive.

She took a train to California, where she was reunited with her sisters. They marveled at her braids, her buckskin dress and tanned skin. They spent many hours trading memories and catching up, at once mourning what might have been as well as celebrating what was. One of her sisters, Elsie, had never married, and the other Anna, was widowed. The three sisters lived together in California for a few years. Elsie became ill and passed away. Hilda and Anna decided then to move back to Michigan. They were both in good health and wanted to be near the distant relatives they had kept in touch with over the long years of separation.

Hilda's son, Runs Fast, had remarried and was quite content in Montana. Hilda knew that she might never see her son again but wanted to go with her sister. She was getting old, and Runs Fast had his own family, so she would not worry about him.

They took the long journey back to Michigan on the train. It was an exhausting journey for the sisters. Upon returning to Michigan, they bought a small house in a town in Southwestern Michigan, called Miller's Creek. It was this town that Sadie had grown up in. It was here that Hilda finally settled, feeling equally at home in the small house she shared with Anna, and in the teepee that she lived in in the summertime, when she couldn't quite bear being indoors all of the time.

## 2

As children, Sadie and Johnny had spent many hours playing in the woods near their home after they had done their chores. Johnny had a few more responsibilities being two years older, so Sadie found herself wandering in the nearby woods and fields often on her own. Her father insisted she take their large mixed breed dog, Tucker, with her when she was by herself. She loved looking for wildflowers and catching little creatures, anything from worms and caterpillars to beetles and butterflies. She never went too far from home, but sometimes she went a little further into the woods than her father liked. He would send Johnny looking for her. She would be found sitting underneath a tree, studying a bug, or examining a flower, Tucker lying nearby, and he would come yelling for her to come home.

On one such day when she had wandered just into the forest, she stopped suddenly as Tucker let loose a deep growl. She knew enough to stop when the dog warned her, so she looked around carefully, wondering what Tucker was upset about. She was surprised to see an old woman with long gray braids and an odd-looking dress just near the edge of the woods. She was wearing a floppy-brimmed hat on her head and was holding a plant in her hand. Sadie was close enough to see that the woman had light blue eyes. Sadie had seen a few Indians before, and knew that they were normally dark-skinned and dark-eyed. Being a child, she didn't question the woman's strange looks. She simply said, "How do you do?"

The woman smiled at Sadie. "I am well, and how do you do, child? Are you lost? Why are you alone?"

"I'm not alone," Sadie responded with a smile of her own. "Tucker is with me."

The old woman smiled even more broadly. "My name is Hilda." She spoke with a strange accent. It sounded like "Heelda".

"My name is Sadie. I'm six years old. This is Tucker, and he's five years old."

Sadie was small for her age, with long dark curly hair and wide sea-green eyes. Hilda had adored her from the time she had laid eyes on her. Sadie was a bright, curious little thing, and Hilda was delighted by the endless questions she had for her. When Hilda found out the child had no mother, she felt even more drawn to her. Sadie brought Hilda home with her to meet her brother and father, who accepted Hilda into their home for supper just as if she were one of the family.

Sadie would go to meet Hilda almost every day during the good weather. Hilda showed her what she was doing, collecting plants and taking them with her in a large bag she carried around her waist. Sadie wanted to know what the names of the plants were, and why Hilda needed them. Hilda explained to her that the plants were medicine, and that they helped to heal people when they were sick.

"I was sick before," said Sadie. "I had a fever and a stuffy nose. And my throat hurt bad."

"I have medicine for that," Hilda said with a smile. "Next time you have a fever, I'll bring you some."

"Can it work for everyone?" asked Sadie, "all the time? 'Cause my brother had one too."

"Yes, child, it works for everyone." Hilda chuckled. "You want to learn more about it? I have many plants to show you."

The friendship between Hilda and Sadie was instant and the bond much like a grandmother and granddaughter. Hilda showed Sadie the odd-looking structure she slept in during the summer months, called a teepee. She had a rack of whittled twigs inside with all manner of plants tied in bundles and hanging upside-down. This was to dry the plants out, and then they would be stored in little jars, or carried with her in small leather bags. Sadie was a quick student, and by the time a year had passed she had learned the names of the plants that helped with fevers, chills, aches, and even some for stomach sickness. Willow bark, slippery elm, yarrow, chamomile, as well as kitchen herbs like thyme, sage, rosemary, and basil were all used for common ailments. Leaves of strawberries, blackberries, and raspberries along with the berries themselves were used in a myriad of different ways, as were the roots of most plants. Sadie loved digging up roots from the plants as much as picking the leaves and the flowers.

As Sadie grew, she assisted Hilda with her plant-gathering and storing, learning how to treat different maladies with the different tinctures and salves that Hilda made. By the time she was ten, her father had given her permission to accompany the old woman when she went to tend to folks who couldn't always get a doctor right away, and both Hilda and Sadie became known for their ability to heal. She carried her own little leather pouch with herbs inside of it, and she knew which plants were used the most for common ailments. She tended her brother and father whenever they had minor injuries or illnesses and did as good of a job as any doctor. She had an impressive knowledge of plant healing and had a way with animals as well as people.

At the age of eleven, Sadie assisted Hilda with a childbirth. One of the young women that lived out in the country had been in labor, and the doctor was away. The woman's husband had come pounding on the door in the middle of the night. Sadie and Johnny went to fetch Hilda and they went to help deliver the baby. Fortunately, it had been a relatively easy birth, though Sadie thought it seemed plenty difficult. It was one of many experiences that she had with Hilda that forged a strong bond between them. The couple's two other children had been captivated by Sadie's ability; she seemed older than her age because of her maturity and manner.

---

As TIME WHEN ON, Sadie became a young woman, and Hilda began to slow down. She had trouble getting around and stopped living in the teepee. When she became more or less stuck inside the small cabin she had shared with her sister, Sadie would visit her nearly every day. The neighbors, especially the poorer ones, had come to count on Sadie for help with their ailments just as they had Hilda when she was younger. They paid her with whatever they could afford, although Sadie didn't expect payment, she would graciously accept what they offered; a homemade pot pie, a chicken, new socks for her father or brother. She loved people and she loved healing. She asked Hilda for advice and shared with her funny stories and some of the goods the people paid her with.

Sadie was the bright spot in Hilda's life. As Hilda's health deteriorated, she looked forward to the daily visits with Sadie and she loved the conversations they had. Hilda had shared the extensive knowledge she had learned in her long and unusual life with her adopted granddaughter and felt that Sadie was going to do marvelous things.

Sadie could tell that Hilda was getting weaker. She was tired frequently and stayed in bed more. During the uncertain days before the United States joined the war in France, Hilda quietly slipped away, peacefully, in her sleep. Sadie barely had time to mourn before she and Johnny made their plans for the immediate future; she would attend nursing school and he would join the Army. She and Hilda had talked about the Great War and Hilda had told Sadie she must use her gift for healing wherever it was needed. Her and Johnny had discussed what they would do if the U.S.

went to war. It was not a decision they had made lightly.

Johnny had come in for breakfast one morning after cleaning out one of the barns on the farm, as they were getting ready to sell it. The horses had been sold to a dear friend and neighbor, and the few cows they had were sold to the butcher shop in Grand Rapids, a city that was around thirty miles away from their small village of Miller's Creek.

Sadie had glanced around their small kitchen, seeing most of their things packed in crates. "Johnny, are you certain that you wish to join the army? You've always wanted to be a farmer. You don't have to be a soldier just because there is a war on." She knew he was going, but the thought filled her with such dread she had to try to get him to change his mind.

Johnny grinned at her with a slightly crooked grin. "Sister, I knew you would try to talk me out of it. You know I have to go. It's my duty." He stopped smiling. "I know you hate the idea. I understand. You know it's the right thing to do."

She nodded. "I know the Germans have to be stopped. They are killing so many innocent people. But I do not have to like it that you are going. You are the only family I have left. It's been so hard since Papa and Hilda have gone."

"It will be all right, Sadie. I promise I will come

back. And if you still doubt that, then you can go over there too and bring me home." He smiled wryly. "No German would dare to stand in your way."

She chuckled at that. She had developed a reputation far and wide for being something of an oddity. Being in the constant company of an old white Indian woman was enough cause for speculation but having a gift for healing was what really set her apart from other girls her age. Folks from all around came to her for medicine and assistance for their ailments. She sighed. She was going to miss being here with their friends and neighbors. She didn't have a lot of friends, but she knew all of the neighbors far and wide and each family was special to her.

Johnny's eyes, similar in color to hers, gleamed with excitement. He finished his breakfast and took his plate to the kitchen sink to wash it. He said then, "Sadie, when I get done with this old war, we will have to decide whether to come back here or settle somewhere else. You know we have to talk about that." They agreed to not discuss the future until after the war. No one could be sure how long it would last, and they were both coming of an age where one or both of them might get married and start their own family. The war had put those things on hold for many people.

Johnny had enlisted, and Sadie had gone to nursing school. Their father had paid the farm off and had set some money aside for his children, and they were able to live comfortably. They had never cared for or had frivolous things, but their needs were always met, and Sadie had enough money to go to school, which she had felt was her calling. Johnny left for the war, and Sadie went to Washington D.C. to train at Walter Reed Hospital.

# 3

A year and a half after they had sold their home, Sadie had gotten the letter she had been dreading from her brother. Johnny was being shipped out to France. He was leaving soon, and she had a few more months of school left. She was working in the hospital with patients that had been in France, and were suffering from wounds that needed long-term care, such as amputees and head wounds. She had seen firsthand the horrors of the gas that the Germans had used against the allied fellows. Those boys suffered long-lasting damage from the foul stuff, whether it was burns on the skin or in the lungs or even blindness. Sadie knew she would be seeing even worse conditions overseas.

She showed the letter to her roommates and fellow

nurses Maude and Sylvia. Maude had two brothers in the army and Sylvia had three. They were dismayed that he was leaving but all three of the girls had planned on going "over there" to be near their brothers.

Sadie had completed the nursing program and all the required field hospital training that they had available. She was so capable that the nursing director sought her out before she was finished and asked her if she would be willing to go in less than a month. Apparently, the need was great. Sadie agreed and made plans to go. She was overjoyed that she would be near her brother again, even though she knew there was a chance she would never see him again; excitement and nervousness warred within her. She felt she was as ready as anyone could be for the field hospital conditions, yet she knew nothing could really prepare her for battlefield conditions. She could not have imagined in her wildest dreams what was in store for her. All she knew for certain was that Johnny was all she had left in the whole world.

# 4

## Brest, France

Sadie could hear the train whistle blowing as it neared the station. She would be boarding before long. She was mentally gathering herself when a voice spoke near her and startled her out of her skin.

"Are you going to one of the field hospitals?" a cheery feminine voice asked. Sadie looked up at a small young woman with bright red hair and vivid blue eyes. She was clutching a small satchel much like Sadie's. Her gaze was fixed hopefully on Sadie's face. Her own face was dotted with freckles and she looked impossibly young.

Sadie stood and smiled questioningly. Before she could speak, the young woman said, "I'm twenty-five!" she chuckled. "Tis the first thing folks notice!"

Sadie smiled more broadly then. "Hello, yes, I am going to a field hospital. I'm not sure which one, but it is a few miles north of Amiens."

The girl looked delighted. "My name is Bridget O'Reilly. I just arrived two days ago about the Masatonia".

"I was on that ship!" Sadie exclaimed with a laugh. "Quite a long voyage for a land girl like myself. I've never been on such a journey, and of course there is more to come."

The girls knew that they had a long train ride in front of them, as well as a truck ride to follow to the front.

"I was never so glad to see land!" said Bridget with a grimace. "Sick as a dog, I was, for the first week!"

"I wasn't seasick, but I sure didn't like the feel of it one bit. All that swaying to and fro." Sadie was so happy to speak to another nurse. She had just had two days of rest, and she was ready to go and was happy to have a companion. Just then, two other girls approached them. One of them was taller than average, near six feet, with a face saved from plainness by a beautiful, angelic smile, and the other was slightly taller than Sadie. She was built solidly and hair a long dark braid wrapped around her head.

"Hello. I am Minnie, and this is Bertie. We are probably going to the same place. The field hospital near Amiens?"

Sadie smiled and said, "Hello, this is Bridget, and I'm Sadie. We are going to a field hospital, I believe it's near Amiens, but I'm not sure. They said there are many hospitals along the front. I know we are going to one of them."

Bertie had a round face that seemed to always be smiling. Her eyes were sparkly and brown, and they almost disappeared into slits when she laughed. She said to the other girls, "Bertha Ann Cunningham, pleased to meet you. My mother did not do well naming us girls. My sisters are called Benjamina and Bethel. My brother's name is Richard."

The girls all laughed at this. Bertie not only had a pleasant, smiling face, but an infectious laugh which made them all giggle harder when they heard it. Sadie's heart was lightened for the moment by the warm friendliness of the other nurses. They shared with each other where they were from, where they had gone to school, and which ship had brought them there. Oddly enough, they had all been on the same ship. Sadie was feeling the loss of her friends in D.C., especially Maude. The long voyage had been monotonous and most of the nurses were preoccupied with what was to come and battling seasickness, so they hadn't really felt like making friends. Now, it seemed like the four of them had known each other longer than a few moments. As they settled in for the train ride, they kept the conversation light and cheerful, each of them knowing in their heart it would be some time before they felt this way again.

5

APRIL 1918

**New York, New York**

Matt Smith boarded the S.S. Argentina with a knot in his stomach. He was finally off to war. He had known it was coming for a long time and had been preparing for months. They had trained as many men, boys, really, as they could in the short time since General John Pershing had formed the American Expeditionary Forces. These soldiers would be trained and shipped overseas as quickly as possible, to relieve the weary Allies in France who had been fighting for three long years.

Matt had been in the Army for several years. At 26,

he was a lieutenant and had more experience than most of the men. He had joined up before he was 18 and had been with the cavalry most of that time. He had chased after Pancho Villa in Mexico in 1916 and was experienced in war already.

He ran his hand across the back of his neck, his only outward sign of agitation. He was a young man of resolve, and he had the nerves of steel that were required to be a combat soldier. He was tall and blond with steady hazel eyes, and a fluid, graceful gait that made him stand out among the rest of the fellows.

Matt could leap onto the back of a horse in one quick, smooth motion; he was one of the best horsemen the Army had ever seen. He and his brother Henry, who was also in the Army, had been raised with horses and they had both learned to ride as soon as they were old enough to hold the saddle horn.

Matt had been with the cavalry until he learned they needed men in the artillery unit. He was good with munitions as well as horses, so he had been transferred to the same unit as his friend Billy Beckett. Billy was a childhood friend of Henry's, but they all had grown up together. As Matt was five years older than the boys, he felt more like an older brother to the gang of boys but was genuinely fond of them all.

As he settled in for the long voyage, he sighed. Like most farm boys, he had never been to sea before. His stomach was already unsettled slightly from nerves, and he knew the three-week long trip across the ocean wasn't going to be easy. Billy had written about seasickness, as he had made the journey over to France a few months before. Being at the mercy of the sea, with no place to escape to was not something that sat easily with Matt. Battling seasickness would weaken the soldiers, and as often as not there were colds and influenzas that spread like wildfire on the crowded ships. The bad influenza going around the world was another insidious enemy, striking the healthy down without warning as well as the frail. He took out his stationary and began writing a letter to his mother. Even though he knew she wouldn't receive it for a while, but he thought that giving himself something to do would be better than sitting doing nothing, and the thought of how pleased she would be to hear from him made him smile just a little. He didn't know when or if he would see his family again. That thought sobered him, and as he began to write, the smile faded from his face.

6

**Field Hospital 5
Near Amiens, France**

Sadie stood in front of the tiny mirror fussing with her hair, trying as usual to tame the unruly mass. She had it braided and pinned up with nearly every pin she had. As soon as she plunked the nurses cap on top of her head a piece of curly hair escaped, and she became annoyed. Her hair was the biggest trial of her life. And she had seen plenty of difficulties. She found another bobby pin and tucked up the offending lock of hair. She heard a stifled giggle and turned with a slightly mutinous look to see Bertie with a hint of mischief in her eyes. Bertie was writing a letter, but she put it away now as they needed to get to work. She and Sadie had been assigned to the same tent, and Bridget and Minnie were just next door. The girls were glad to have their new friends as roommates.

"Are you nearly ready, Sadie?" she asked sweetly.

"How do you keep all that hair so neat?" Sadie asked, eying Bertie's long hair that was so tidy for its length.

"Mine isn't nearly as curly as yours," Bertie tried to keep a straight face, to her credit. "Your hair is lovely, dear, truly."

Sadie sighed. "Let's go."

When the women had first found out that they were all going to the same hospital, they had been grateful to have found one another. They had much in common. Having lost everyone dear to her except her brother, Sadie had come here to France to be near him. Bertie's finance had been killed in the war and she had gone into nursing to fill the void in her life and to contribute to the war effort. Bridget was engaged but hadn't heard from her fiancé for over a year. Minnie had seven brothers, two of which had been killed, four were still fighting, and one was at home looking after their elderly parents.

There had been seventy nurses on the train. When the women had arrived the night before, they had only time for a cursory look around the hospital. They had only seen the four tents that held the patients, from the outside, and their sleeping quarters. They had walked past several other large tents but needed rest first, said the Miss Frain, the nurse in charge. The nurses had been delayed an entire day as the train had to stop at the site of a skirmish that took place along the tracks. The Germans had tried to steal some supplies that were coming in for the Allies and had met with fierce resistance. The nurses had been forced to disembark and spent the day in the small town near the railway so the tracks could be cleared.

As the train began rolling through the countryside again, the girls were stunned into silence by the carnage that lay all around. Giant holes left by the mortars scarred the beautiful green fields, pieces of wagons and some of the supplies that had been lost were strewn about. Far worse, bodies of men and horses were scattered everywhere. By the time they had transferred from the train to the army trucks and finished the journey to the hospital the women were exhausted.

The first person the girls met was Nurse Isadora Frain, a matronly woman around sixty years of age, tall and stoutly built. She had steely blue eyes, and a formidable expression that suggested she was not used to smiling. She was in charge of all of the nurses at the hospital. Miss Frain told them to get a solid night's sleep and meet her in the overflow tent for a tour of the entire grounds. They would meet the doctors and other staff in the afternoon, and the next morning report for duty.

Before they began the tour of the hospital, Nurse Frain gathered the girls together for a briefing in the meeting tent. They would be split into four groups, with each group being shown around by an experienced nurse. Many of the nurses that were here already were nuns, and all of them had careworn expressions that told the story of what they had seen in this place, how hard they had been working, and the resignation that came with dealing with death on a daily basis. Sadie wondered if they would all have that same look after a few months here.

They knew what to expect to some degree; they had been told about the clearing stations at the front that treated the wounded temporarily and then sent them on to the field hospital. There were a few small medical stations scattered up and down the front that were staffed with a few men for anyone who had been cut off from their unit or displaced civilians who might need help. Some of the medical stations were fluid; that is, they would pack up and follow the battle line in order to stay as close as was necessary to treat the injured as quickly as possible.

Sadie's group started with the supply tent, which they were instructed was always to be kept meticulously clean and organized so that everything that was needed was in easy reach. There were some volunteer girls that spent their whole days washing and rolling up bandages. They were set up on the outskirts of the camp, with giant caldrons to boil the bandages in and lines to dry them, and Sadie could see buckets of bloodied bandages off to one side, and stacks of clean, rolled bandages on the other. Long clotheslines were strung along the edge of the last row of tents, with hundreds if not thousands of bandages and bedsheets hung out in the breeze.

The next tent they saw was the mess tent. It was long and large and sat around one hundred people at a time. The nurses would take all of their meals here or bring their meals to their tents if they wanted privacy. There were orderlies and a few nurses having lunch at the moment. Some of them had the same weary looks that the nurses Sadie had seen earlier. There were some light-hearted conversations going on, but Sadie could see they all looked very tired.

The overflow tent was used for recreation, as it could be had, as well as an emergency ward if they had a large influx of wounded. They had only needed as such once since the hospital had been there. It was also very large and could hold up to one hundred and fifty beds.

The new nurses were going to be shown the tents where the wounded soldiers were next. As they approached the first one, Sadie, Bridget, Minnie, and Bertie exchanged glances that told one another that the nerves came jumping back, just for a moment. What would they see inside? Would their training be enough? Each one felt a weight on her shoulders; would she be enough?

Before they even entered the tent, they could smell that the air inside was think with the stench of putrid wounds. The girls steeled themselves and followed Nurse Frain inside.

This tent contained the greatest variety of wounds; cuts, burns, gunshot wounds, general trauma, shell shock, head wounds. Some of the poor men with deathly ill with infected wounds. The nurses discovered that this tent was the most complex in that they had to monitor and record vitals for a myriad of different types of injuries. They were to carefully watch for signs of infection, change dressings, clean wounds, and bathe the patients, as well as be prepared to call for an orderly if the patient became violent and the nurse couldn't restrain him, or in the event of death. If all the orderlies were busy or if it were nighttime and a patient died, the nurse was responsible for handling the body.

They left the first tent and entered the second, which was for the victims of gas. The mustard, chlorine, and phosgene gases that were used against the allies were hideous, that the girls all knew. But seeing one or two patients during their schooling was so much different than seeing scores of men with eyes bandaged, gasping for each breath, or covered in red, weeping blisters. Sadie could hear a few of the men drawing wet, heavy breaths, and she swallowed hard in a moment of sheer panic. How terrifying it must be for these poor boys to be struggling so hard for each draw of air. She steeled herself as she often did when confronted with people in pain and misery. She had learned from a very young age that she needed to remain calm in order to be the most help to someone. One young man caught her eye. Dear Lord, he was young. He looked to be fifteen years old at most. She wondered if that were possible. She thought of Johnny, and asked God to watch over him. The stench of gangrene lung was prevalent. Sadie had been warned of this, and between the men's symptoms and the smell, she knew that this was the very thing she had feared. It was very distressing. Growing up she dealt with an occasionally infection, but Hilda had seen to it that most wounds never degenerated to that point, if they got to the person in time, that was.

The moved on to the amputee tent. Sadie and the others saw around forty men, all with limbs missing, lined up in two long rows with an aisle in between, as well as a goodly amount of space around the beds. This was to make it easier for the wounded men to move about with crutches and wheelchairs. Sadie could tell that the hospital staff was meticulous about cleanliness. The bandages all looked to be clean and fresh. The nurses had been told that many of the field hospitals were struggling to keep up with the number of wounded coming in, so they were all relieved to see that this was not the case here, at least not at the moment.

Sadie caught the eye of a young soldier with a missing leg. He had bright blue eyes and bright red hair. He cheekily winked at her and smiled. He looked so innocent that she laughed softly. These fellows all looked to be in rough shape, but they were being well-cared for. She had heard about conditions on the front and hoped it wouldn't be as bad as all that. From what she understood, this was a well-run, established hospital that hadn't had problems so far getting supplies, although they could be scarce at times. She was quite pleased to see this; she'd had no idea what to expect but had heard that some of the hospitals were badly understaffed and ill-equipped. It couldn't be predicted where the worst of the battles would be fought, and sometimes patients had to be transported farther than was ideal to find a hospital with room enough for them.

The soldiers all looked worn down in one way: their uniforms were filthy and becoming ragged. There were no spare uniforms to be had, and because the men had rare opportunity to bathe, they had another enemy to fight that was a plague: lice. The men were constantly tormented by the tiny devils. They didn't have a change of clothes, so if they passed through a hospital, at the very least their clothes would be washed at least once while they were there. On the front line, the men had little water at their disposal.

The last tent was for respiratory patients. There could be gas patients that were transferred over here from another tent, or it could be pneumonia, or the dreaded influenza that was spreading like wildfire around the world. This tent was divided into two sections. The influenza patients were kept at the opposite end of the tent that had respiratory patients. There were many empty beds in this tent at present, as the hospital anticipated an outbreak of flu at any time. The girls noticed the large canvas divider that was rolled up and fastened at the top with rope. If the influenza beds became occupied, the canvas would be dropped, and it would partition off the flu patients.

As they finished their tour of the patients' tents, they walked around the entire encampment to the outside of it, where there was a smaller tent with a sign that said, "Apothecary" posted in front. Here they stored all of the plant medicines; salves, tinctures, powders, and the plants themselves. From the living plants they could make poultices and they were instructed that those with the knowledge would be charged with foraging for more plants whenever they were able. Sadie had learned many ways to heal, beyond nursing school. Hilda, her childhood mentor and friend, had taught her everything she knew about healing with plant medicine.

After they were back in the recreation/overflow tent, Nurse Frain, the nurse in charge, spoke to them briefly about where they would find their duties for the day.

"You will be assigned a tent each day and are to ask the charge nurse for your patients. You will be assigned a share of the patients but be prepared for the possibility of being called away to help elsewhere if need be. We will on occasion get a large number of incoming soldiers and might need help in one area more than another." She paused for a moment, looked down on her notepad, and then said, "Sadie Prentiss."

"Yes, ma'am?" Sadie stepped forward.

"Your file says that you have excellent skills in the surgery and a wealth of knowledge in plant medicine."

Sadie nodded, feeling a little self-conscious. Nurse Frain continued. "Tomorrow morning after you check in, I'd like you to take a look at our supplies in the apothecary. Perhaps Bridget could accompany you?" Bridget replied, "Of course, ma'am."

"We will be getting to meet the doctors in a moment. Sadie, Bridget, Bertie, you all have assisted in surgery, so I would like you specially to take some time to speak with the doctors so they can get to know you a little bit. Fortunately for now we are not too busy with new patients so while we have that advantage, we shall introduce you to the rest of the staff."

The proceeded to the surgery tent, where they were met by four doctors. These were the doctors on staff today, there was a total of eight doctors, and they were all good, according to Nurse Frain.

Sadie was immediately struck by one of the doctors; he was young a handsome with piercing green eyes and thick light brown hair. He was British and his name was Dr. Roger Fielding. Dr. Waverly, the next doctor, was around 30, average height, his face distinguished by thick bushy sideburns and a nearly hairbrushed sized mustache. He had gentle, kind, blue eyes. Sadie like him right away. Then came Dr. Murphy, who was handsome in a more sophisticated way, almost fatherly, his face lined with character. The last doctor was Dr. Carter, who had perhaps the most impassive face Sadie had ever seen. His eyes glittered with something that looked like annoyance, or was it disapproval? Sadie thought to herself that this doctor might prove to be troublesome. She had met doctors back in Washington that had underestimated her because of her appearance, and she hadn't care for it one bit. Having always been small for her age, she had always had to work harder and be more persistent in order for people to take her seriously.

After he introduced himself to all of them, Dr. Carter said, "I expect you ladies to remember who is in charge here."

Nurse Frain looked side-eyed at him and raised an eyebrow, then moved on.

"Drs. Fielding and Dr. Waverly are mostly in the surgery when we have injured men come in. Dr. Murphy is an expert in infections and Dr. Carter is a respiratory doctor, but all four of them do everything and most of them are Army doctors. Dr. Fielding is our only civilian doctor. We do tolerate civilian doctors fairly well if they are qualified." Everyone snickered at this and Sadie decided that she liked Nurse Frain. "Lastly, every three days one of our doctors accompanies one of the medics to the front line clearing station.

The doctor on this detail will be present to apply first aid to those in immediate danger during a battle. It is the most dangerous time for our doctors. He stays three days, then he is replaced by another. This rotation continues during the entire course of the war. Our Doctor Townsend is currently on the front. He is due back tomorrow, so you will meet him then." She paused. "Any questions for our Doctors?" She looked down the line of nurses. "How about you Doctors? Any questions for our nurses?"

Dr. Carter said, "I'm assuming these nurses have experience with battle wounds?" His gaze flicked over the young women with impatience, as if they were inconveniencing him by being there. Sadie felt a prickle of annoyance.

"Yes, Doctor, all of our nurses have seen battle wounds. Nurse Prentiss is actually our youngest nurse, but she is also the most calm and steady under duress in the surgery." Sadie felt a mild heat in her cheeks at this but maintained her composure. She didn't like Dr. Carter so far. He should know that the nurses would not have been sent all this way without proper training.

"Erm... my apologies, Miss Frain," said Dr. Carter. "I misspoke. It just appears that some of them are so young."

"I'm twenty-five." Bridget muttered indignantly.

SADIE SPENT the day familiarizing herself with the small tent with its shelves of carefully labeled jars containing salves and dried herbs and tinctures. The back of the tent was partitioned off with a large section of canvas, and behind it was a variety of potted plants. Many of them were species Sadie was familiar with, a few she was not. The canvas was rolled up and tied at the top during the day so the plants could get sunlight and air circulation. At night, the piece of canvas was unrolled and secured at the bottom.

She found a book with everything carefully logged. She spent the next few hours showing Bridget some of the most commonly used remedies and made meticulous notes of her own. She didn't need to write down things for herself, but for those who came after her. She had been healing with plants for most of her life, and besides, the person who had made the notebook in the apothecary had done an excellent job of cataloging the items that were at hand.

She and Bridget chatted while they worked, and Sadie found that Bridget was bright and curious, and absorbed information very quickly. They had gone through most of the small tent's contents by lunchtime and were ready to go see how their friends had fared.

They got their food onto trays and went and found

a seat next to Bertie, who was chatting with an orderly, a red-haired giant named Richard, who for more than one reason went by the nickname of Red. Not only did he have fiery red hair that would serve as a beacon to anyone lost nearby, but he blushed and flushed more than anyone Sadie had ever seen. She caught Bridget's eye and they both snickered.

"Thankfully, it's been quiet the last few days," Red was saying. "You ladies have a bit of time to learn the ropes, hopefully before we get an influx of wounded." Then he added with a blush, "Not that you need to learn anything...I mean..."

Bertie piped up, "Oh, goodness, Red, calm yourself!" It was like they had known each other forever.

The girls laughed. Red was light-hearted and jolly, not what they would have expected in this place that saw such devastation. It was exactly what they needed.

As the next few days were quiet around the grounds of the hospital, each of the new nurses was able to spend time in each of the four tents, and they were given a look inside of the surgery tent as well. Sadie and Bridget had both had surgical training so they were shown by Nurse Frain and another nurse how they would be assisting when needed. The procedures were done almost the same way as back in the hospitals where the girls had trained, but only when time permitted. When there was a flood of patients coming in, there was not always time for proper protocol. Nurse Frain looked at both girls, then said,

"It may come down to the nurses quickly having to administer anesthetic and orderlies hold the patient down so the doctor can remove a limb quickly if necessary. It gets very messy and very traumatic, as I'm sure you can imagine." Nurse Frain looked at them with a look that told them they could not imagine. Sadie and Bridget were both competent in surgery, and they knew that they were going to be tried severely in the days and weeks to come.

---

CHAOS CAME in the early hours of the next morning. Sadie was startled awake by loud voices rushing past the nurses' quarters, calling for all nurses and orderlies to meet at the triage tent. She and Bertie quickly dressed and pinned up their hair and ran out to meet the ambulances. As soon as Sadie exited her tent, she ran smack into someone. It was Dr. Carter.

"Nurse, follow me," he commanded. Sadie hurried after him, her stomach flipping and flopping. What was she doing here? She didn't know if she was prepared for this. She forced her thoughts to become more positive and followed Dr. Carter. He led her not to the triage but to the gas tent. There were approximately twenty new injured men in the tent already.

Dr. Carter stopped at the first bed. "These fellows came in all at once; they're all gas victims so you'll have to triage them here. He gestured to the soldier's bandaged-wrapped head. "Unwrap, clean up the best you can, re-bandage, write the number on the board, move on," he said curtly.

"Yes, sir," Sadie met his hard-eyed glance briefly and got to it. The sound of men gasping, coughing, wheezing was all around her. Sadie steeled herself and began unwrapping the first man's head. He was young, the bandage was stained with blood and something else, she wasn't sure what it was. She threw the soiled bandage in a bucket next to the bed and gently and quickly cleaned the young man's face. After wiping away the grit and grime, she applied ointment to the burns and his eyes and re-bandaged him before writing a number on the small chalkboard above the bed. She moved on to the next man.

She spoke softly to the men as she worked, explaining what she was doing, doing her best to calm each man, most of whom were shaky and terrified. When she was finished with each patient, she wrote either a 1, which meant immediate intervention was necessary, 2, wounds which required immediate attention was needed but not life-threatening injuries, or 3, wounds that were not life-threatening.

Sadie didn't think Dr. Carter's expression ever changed. She could tell that he was efficient and very competent and that encouraged her. She began unwrapping the next man's face and stopped, her stomach dropping to the floor. She could see right away that one of the young man's eyes was missing and a large piece of his face was badly torn and burned. She noticed there was blood coming out of his ear.

She looked helplessly at Dr. Carter. He sighed very slightly and shook his head. "Move on," he said quietly.

The next patient appeared to be in better condition. She said, "Hello, I am Sadie, and I am going to be your nurse. I'll be unwrapping your bandage, examining your eyes, and taking care of you. How are you feeling, sir?"

The young soldier had ruddy cheeks and very blue eyes. She was struck at how beautiful his blue eyes were and dismayed at how there was not a trace of white left in them. They were pure red, and watering constantly. In addition, the skin was blistered around his eyes, but that seemed to be the extent of his injury. Sadie was hopeful that he would be able to see again. Sometimes the gas blinded them permanently, and sometimes it was temporary. She applied some salve to his eyes, squeezed his hand gently, and said, "You're going to be just fine, soldier." She wrote a 1 on his board and moved on. The next fellow was around thirty, tall and thin, and when he spoke, he had a British accent. He had just returned to the fight after a lengthy stint in the hospital, and his unit had the misfortune of getting gassed immediately as soon as he returned to battle. His voice was raspy as he told the sad tale.

"Thanks, mum. 'Adn't a chance, we dint. Buggers caught us in a shell-'ole." He had a slight tremor in his hand as he reached up to touch his head. "Hit me head, too." He smiled then. "Guess I'd a figured I'd be dead b'now."

Sadie smiled gently at the man. "My name is Sadie. I'll have the doctor over as soon as I can. What is your name, sir?"

"Randolph, mum." She patted his shoulder, wrote a 1 on the board, and moved to the next man. And so, it went for several hours. They brought a few more men into the tent, but most of them had been seen. Sadie could tell who had gotten the worst of it. Blistered faces, reddened eyes, ears, necks, hands, all covered with varying degrees of redness or weeping sores. A few of them were unresponsive after a couple of hours of snuffling, wet-sounding attempts to breathe. Sadie was devastated that they couldn't do anything for those men. Someone's son. Someone's husband. Someone's father. Who was looking after her brother? Was he even still alive? She put the thought out of her mind and concentrated on the task at hand. Some of them would be sent home, and she wondered at how they would survive a truck ride, a train ride, or a voyage across the sea, in the condition they were in. As soon as it was possible, the men would have to be transported out of the hospital here to make room for more incoming wounded. Whenever there was a battle, there was a wave of new arrivals.

Sadie pulled a sheet up over the face of a young man who had just lost his life. She added his name to the list of the deceased. It would be another letter she had to write to another family who had just lost their loved one. Most of the fellows had pictures in their pockets of their sweetheart, or siblings, or sometimes mothers. Sadie drew a deep, fortifying breath. Her throat ached with unshed tears.

At the end of her first day in the gas tent, Sadie half-heartedly ate her supper. She had been working for thirteen hours. She stumbled into her tent, changed into her nightclothes, and fell into a deep, dreamless sleep.

SADIE, Bertie, Bridget, and Minnie were playing cards in the meeting tent. Bridget said ladies didn't play cards, but she said it with a gleam in her eye as she sat down to play. Bertie giggled her way through the game. Her rusty-haired orderly, Red, was at the other end of the tent with some friends also playing cards. The other girls were amused at how outrageously Bertie and Red flirted. They spent as much time together as was decent.

Since Minnie was quiet most of the time, Sadie was delighted to learn that she loved playing pranks on people. It probably came from having seven brothers. She was not afraid of spiders, frogs, or snakes. She had howled with laughter when she had frightened Bridget "nearly to death" by propping up a dead spider on poor Bridget's pillow. It stood almost an inch off the pillow with its legs standing up as if it were alive, and they had all heard Bridget let out an unearthly scream, followed by Minnie chortling. Bertie and Sadie had come running to find a spluttering, red-faced Bridget and Minnie lying on the bed, clutching her stomach in a fit of laughter, tears rolling down her cheeks. Sadie and Bertie found it hilarious, and soon Bridget, being a good sport, laughed as well, although she swore revenge on Minnie.

# 7

Dr. Fielding was showing Sadie and Bridget around the surgery. Both girls had come highly recommended from their nursing school for being highly competent in surgery. Sadie had such an unusual wealth of medical knowledge in general that she would be indispensable at the hospital. Roger felt incredibly grateful that God had brought these two highly qualified, if young, nurses to help in this terrible place. At thirty-one, he had been in this war for three years already. He had seen the best and worst of humanity in this place.

He had felt called to come here when the war started, as the need for doctors was great and immediate. The war had started so suddenly, and the sheer number of men needed for such a war was so overwhelming that the amount of medical support needed was tremendous right from the beginning. Medical school hadn't prepared him for the trauma he faced at the front. He was an excellent surgeon and had come to France with nearly eight years of experience in the hospital in London. The conditions on the front were completely different than anything he'd ever seen before. The lack of cleanliness, the number of patients and the shortage of supplies and staff had caused him to think outside of the box and push the parameters of regulations in such a way that his younger self would never have believed. The terrible wounds that the soldier had were so varied that it was hard for any of the hospitals to effectively treat all of them. Doing the best that they could often had to be enough.

"Ladies, you both are welcome here, believe me. I hear you have been settling in all right? It got lively the other morning, hmm?" He turned to Sadie with a look of admiration.

"Miss Prentiss, you are twenty-one years of age, and you have quite a reputation already with the doctors and other staff at Walter Reed as being very steady under pressure."

"I have a strong constitution," replied Sadie. Her resilience was nothing to her; it was who she was, and it was all she had ever known. She was more surprised at women who grew silly and faint over everything than she was with her own "stoic" nature.

Roger glanced around the surgery and then looked at Bridget and Sadie with eyes that were slightly sad for a moment and more than a little weary. "I don't know if you can imagine this place soaked with blood, but it gets bad on occasion. It happens very quickly, when we get bombarded with patients, there is simply too many to save, injuries that cannot be helped, or if they were patched quickly at the battle site sometimes there is already infection." He paused for a moment, then indicated the twenty operating tables. "We have twenty, but we only have six doctors at the most at any given time. We have had our surgery nurses suture, remove shrapnel, administer anesthetic and so on. Sometimes we may need more from you."

Bridget and Sadie both nodded.

"Dr. Fielding," began Bridget.

"Roger," please. "We don't stand on formality with those who we get bloodied up to our neck with."

"Roger," Bridget said, looking up at him directly, "we will do anything in our ability to help save lives. You won't find us squeamish."

Sadie nodded. "We understand that we haven't faced battle conditions. But for as long as I can remember, I have been stitching people up, and Bridget for a good long time too, I understand." The girls had formed a fast friendship and felt as if they had known each other for years instead of weeks.

Roger looked down at the two women who were quite diminutive in stature and smiled. "Do you think you can hold a fellow down if you need to if we don't have time to sedate him?"

Bridget let out a chuckle at this. "Dr.-Roger, sir, I can wrestle a four-hundred-pound pig to the ground, I am sure I can handle a wee man." Her Irish came out a little more often than not and Sadie found it endearing.

"Sadie? I'm assuming you're strong as well?"

"Yes, sir, quite." Sadie smiled. "I have been tending sick people and animals since I was eight. I took care of my father for two years before he passed."

She thought that Dr. Fielding was very handsome, and as she glanced at Bridget, she appeared to have noticed as well. Her cheeks were slightly pink. Although it was greatly frowned upon, relationships did form among doctors and nurses as well as soldiers and nurses.

Roger continued, "When there are men bleeding everywhere, and it's loud and confusing and there is no time to think, you need to make decisions immediately to save as many as possible. I don't mean to mislead you; we are more often than not adequately able to tend to whoever comes in. However, sometimes there are just too many and we can't help them all. The worst part is when we patch them up and help them heal and they go back to the front and end up right back here again, or worse. This has been going on three years already. It never stops. And as if that were not bad enough, now we have the influenza as well.

"Tomorrow I will be relieving Dr. Townsend, so he will be returning, and you will meet him. He is a younger fellow, like me. We have a day to rest after our time at the front, then we are back on the surgery schedule. Should either of you need anything, you have only to ask."

He went on to explain to them that they had a dozen or so combat-surgery nurses but that they had often worked without enough rest so Bridget and Sadie could be added in to help alleviate the burden.

---

THE NURSES SPENT the next several days tended to their patients. They held their hands while they died and wrote letters to next of kin. Some of the men were blinded from the gas, and Sadie soon realized that absence of sight brought about panic and despair more than almost anything else. Sadie tried to remember all their names. She spoke soothingly to them and tried to give them hope, the one thing they needed. She knew this was literally the darkest hour any of them would ever face, and that they could go forward from here and heal. She enjoyed this aspect of nursing; her naturally optimistic nature served her well here. The soldiers loved her for both her pretty face and her sunny disposition.

Sadie and Bridget spent a few hours in the surgery with Dr. Townsend, another handsome doctor with blond hair and light blue eyes. He was young, as Roger had told them, but also weary looking, especially around the eyes, as if he had seen too many things he should not have. The patients in the surgery were there mostly for infections that needed to be cleaned out and restitched. It was a miserable thing for the soldiers, suffering the pain and discomfort from the infection. They often had fevers, which Sadie treated with her plant teas along with aspirin, sometimes in place of it. All in all, it was a brief interlude of quiet.

8
---

Most of the nurses had become very good friends. Much to the delight of Sadie and Bertie, they were moved out of their tent into a larger one and joined by Bridget and Minnie. Their original lodgings were being given to several recently arrived doctors that each got a tent to himself. Which was just fine with the girls. They had the best time chatting in the morning and in the evenings. The commiserated with each other and shared their burdens and joys. Minnie entertained them with stories of her brothers and all of their pranks. She was nearly six feet tall and said she was the shortest one in the family.

Bertie had a sadder tale. She had been engaged to be married. Her finance had been called to war just a few weeks before their wedding day. He had special experiencing with map-making and his skill was desperately needed. He was killed almost immediately when he arrived in France.

Bertie had decided that action was necessary for her to survive. She had attended nursing school and signed up for the overseas position as soon as she could. No one could immediately see the pain behind her merry brown eyes and irrepressible good nature. She was thirty, the oldest of the four of them. She was much like an older sister to them.

Bridget told them about her young man in the Army. They were also engaged, but she hadn't heard from him in over a year. They had written a few times, then the letters had stopped. She kept going as if she was still engaged, because that was what she had to do.

They were discussing this very fact one evening when they heard a loud voice rushing past their tent, shouting, "All available nurses to emergency stations!" Each nurse had been assigned an emergency station to present to when the ambulances came in. Since the girls had just changed into their nightclothes, they hurried back into their uniforms, hastily pinning up their hair and foregoing their caps in their rush to meet the ambulances.

There were at least six ambulances that Sadie could see. She knew that the most critically wounded would be aboard the trucks and that there would be horse-drawn wagons bringing additional patients later, as they took longer to arrive. Sadie had been assigned to surgery that night, so she hurried to the operating tent. Her breath caught in her throat when she followed an orderly inside. Each table had a man on it already, and more were being brought in. It was a nightmare of bloodied, moaning, screaming men and doctors barking orders and orderlies and nurses scurrying about. Sadie followed the instructions of the orderly she had come in with. She pulled out the previously readied trays of surgical instruments and quickly distributed them to several of the doctors. There was another nurse doing the same.

Sadie could see more men being brought in and laid on the ground around the outer edges of the tent.

"Here, Sadie!" Dr. Carter called to her. She saw a man lying on the table with a stump where one leg should be wrapped in a field bandage. He clearly had needed a field amputation to save his life, and though the bandage looked tidy enough, it was soaked through with blood and the man was deathly pale and trembling badly. Dr. Carter was quickly unwrapping the dripping bandage. This man might not even survive the next minute. "He's unconscious," Dr. Carter said. "Next patient." He gestured to the table next to them. While he continued to work on the unresponsive man, for the moment, he told Sadie to begin removing the next patient's clothing so she could clean his wounds and triage him. She knew he must be in bad condition to be in the surgery tent. She saw in a moment that he had a deep wound in his chest and his body was riddled with shrapnel. She began packing his wound with gauze, noting Dr. Fielding approaching the table. He took over for her with the gaping hole in the man's chest and asked her to begin picking out the larger pieces of metal. As he worked on stitching the hole closed, he instructed her to clean the wounds she could as quickly as possible and then move on to the next patient. Sadie was getting warm and she could see the tent was quickly become overcrowded. When she got to the next man, she could see his arm was hanging at a very odd angle. She saw the shattered bone in his upper arm and said loudly, "Here, please!" Dr. Carter materialized at her side. His surgical apron was covered in blood.

He glanced around for an orderly, seeing no one free, tersely asked Sadie, "Can you administer anesthetic?" She nodded and before Dr. Carter could blink, she was at the task, and the man was unconscious. He was impressed in spite of himself and his normal tolerance for young nurses. She was very steady and calm, with none of the silly foolishness he saw in so many girls. She assisted him perfectly and had the man's fresh stump neatly bandaged in no time so he could move on to the next man.

Sadie was also covered in blood, and other things by now. She could smell the coppery tang of blood in the air. The tables ran with blood, the ground was covered in it, and there were growing pails of limbs and bloodied rags all around.

"Hold him!" Dr. Carter barked at an orderly who was trying to keep a soldier on the table that was determined to get off from it. He was out of his mind with pain. Not only did he have a mangled arm, but his face was burned as well, and he was bleeding from many wounds all over his body. He was young, she could see freckles standing out on his pale face. He was also very thin, as so many of them were. Sadie quickly ran to the man's side, spoke soothingly to him, holding his good hand, calming him nearly instantly and the orderly was able to administer the chloroform so the doctor could begin the amputation.

Removing a limb did not take long; the complicated part of that particular surgery came in the recovery. Keeping the men infection-free was the most difficult job of any hospital staff. The grueling task before them all right now was to remove dirt and debris from the wounds as well as tend to the burns, stitch wounds closed and see to each man quickly, so they could work on each of them before their time ran out.

The next poor fellow was missing most of his uniform already, so they had little to cut off from him. He very clearly had one arm missing and he was thrashing around so badly there were two orderlies holding him down. "Nurse!" Dr. Carter shouted. "Chloroform!" Sadie quickly administered the anesthetic to the black-haired lad as the men held him down. Again, she noted how young these soldiers were. This young man was bleeding from a cut on his head as well.

"Sir? His head…" Dr. Carter glanced around, and said, "Will you stitch it please, Nurse?"

Sadie got to it immediately. She had fourteen stitches in place before the doctor was finished with his amputation.

And on it went, soldier after soldier, on through the night, the smell of blood in her nostrils was so familiar she thought she might never be able to forget it as long as she lived.

Dr. Carter looked down at the tiny woman in front of him and said, "Nurse Prentiss. Thank you. You've done well." Sadie looked up from the man whose body had they had been picking shrapnel out of for three hours, and was surprised to see that she, Dr. Carter, and their patient were the only ones left in the surgery.

The rest had been moved into the tent with the other surgical patients.

"Thank you, sir," Sadie said quietly. "Will he live?"

"I believe he will. I have to," said Dr. Carter. "Otherwise, why are we here?"

Sadie was surprised to hear such a philosophical question from Dr. Carter. He looked exhausted, and she was beginning to feel the same. She looked at Dr. Carter and asked, "Is it like this often?"

Dr. Carter looked at her with a slight softening in his stern expression. "It can be, but most often, it is not. Now, you have done exceedingly well here tonight. Go and take a good long rest."

Sadie nodded, said, "Thank you, sir." Then she smiled slightly and said, "You too, sir," and went to wash up. When she finished, she found that it was breakfast time. She had worked completely through the night. She quickly ate some eggs and toast and then went to fall exhausted into bed.

A few hours later she awoke to find Bertie standing next to her bed. "How are you feeling this afternoon?" Bertie giggled. "You were certainly busy last night. Word around the hospital is that Dr. Carter thinks pretty highly of you."

Sadie flushed a little. "I was only doing my job." She looked around. "What time is it?" She felt as if she had sand under her eyelids.

Bertie said, "It's time for supper. They brought 52 men here last night. We lost five almost right off. I just saw the fellow with all the shrapnel. He is doing all right. He's in some awful pain, but fortunately morphine is plentiful at the moment. Here anyway. There are shortages here and there along the front." She paused for a moment, then said, "Minnie lost another brother. He was in the group that came in last night."

"Where were they fighting?" Sadie asked, trying to wake up.

"They were about twenty miles from here. You know how loud the guns have been lately? The Germans were pushing our boys back and they had them trapped in a small field and surrounded on all sides. It's miraculous that any of them got away. Someone managed to break through the line and get around behind the Germans and drew fire away from our boys. That was when they got the wounded out." Bertie rubbed the back of her neck. "Anyway, Nurse Frain says you are not to report to duty until tomorrow morning."

# 9

Three more men died over the course of the next few days. Sadie spent most of her time administering herbal tea and poultices to the patients. Chamomile calmed them some and helped them sleep, water plantain, parsley, mint, and goldenrod for digestive issues. Lamb's ear, cattail, self-heal and others Sadie had learned about from her time with Hilda helped with bleeding wounds and burns. There were many pots of aloe vera kept in a warm spot that were crucial in treating the skin blisters and burns caused by the gas and bursting shells. Gunpowder burns from misfiring weapons caused severe burns sometimes. There were so many ways to be harmed in the fight.

Bridget was a huge help to her and had an amazing ability to remember each plant and what it treated most effectively. She helped Sadie keep meticulous records, for just as with aspirin and morphine, too much of plant medicine could be harmful as well.

There were always ointments and tinctures to be made, keeping up with the demand was an undertaking that there never seemed enough time for. Whenever the girls had a couple of hours to themselves or a day off, they liked to go out foraging for wild plants to replenish their supply. Sadie taught Bridget, Minnie, and Bertie how Hilda had taught her; gather the plants carefully and only every third one, so that there would be plenty for the next time they were needed. Sadie thought lovingly of everything Hilda had been to her; healer, mother, teacher, friend. She could never have dreamed that her odd lifestyle would have helped save so many lives. She was grateful for her ability to heal and for the lifetime of knowledge that Hilda had imparted to her. She missed the old woman.

For the hundredth time, she wondered how Johnny was. The last letter she had received from him had been brief but reassuring; at least that he was still alive. She wondered if he had been wounded or killed since then. Or even worse, suffering from shellshock, the battle trauma that left so many incoherent, shaking violently, some for the rest of their lives. She had seen the blank stares and seen men jump under beds when the big guns got close. Many of them never recovered.

The ones that endured this indignity ended up in institutions where doctors attempted to solve the puzzle of this malady. Understandably, the men couldn't get over killing their fellow man, and constantly not knowing when the end would come for them or their fellow soldiers wore them down and damaged some of them beyond repair. Some of them came back slowly, others were merely a shadow of their former selves.

Sadie said a prayer for Johnny. She said another for the rest of the boys. Then she said a prayer for herself, and the other nurses, and doctors. She prayed that God would stop this misery before any more lives were lost. She prayed for Johnny every time she thought of him. He was all she had left in this world.

---

THE GIRLS WERE out foraging one morning when they heard a loud shout coming from the hospital camp. They ran back to see what was happening.

## 10

### MAY 1918

Matt was running as fast as he could. His company was currently under heavy fire, fighting for their lives and for the precious supplies they were transferring to another company that was pinned down. The Germans were constantly trying to sabotage their efforts to get supplies through. They attacked the trains themselves, and when that failed, they went after the wagons transporting the much-needed food and medical supplies to the front. They succeeded in destroying one wagon and killing a few men, but most got through. Now, Matt and his friends were fleeing away from the enemy and drawing them further away from the Allies.

Matt had been with Billy Beckett for a time, and then he'd been transferred to the $120^{th}$ where he'd been needed for his skills with horses. He and a half dozen others rode up and down the line of supply wagons, keeping watch for the Germans. Matt's brother Henry was working supplies around here somewhere, and Matt had hoped to run into him, but it didn't happen, so he thought at least he'd be able to ask someone if they'd seen him. But that didn't happen either. Somehow, the Germans had gotten between the cavalry and the supplies, and Matt along with a few others had distracted the enemy, drawing their fire away from the precious barrels of food and medicine. The Germans began shooting at the horses, dropping them from under their riders. Matt was one such victim of this tactic. One moment he was flying along on the back of his mount and the next he was being thrown through the air. A lifetime of riding experience had him rolling as he hit the ground. He summersaulted a few times and landed up and running. It was pitch black. He prayed he wouldn't break an ankle running through the dark. Then he saw the tree line of the woods off to the side. Whenever there was a flash of light from the mortars exploding all around him, he could see a few of his friends' faces on the edge of the woods.

In the flares of light Matt could see their faces, contorted with intense emotion as they shouted encouragement to him and the others that were running alongside him. He was about fifty yards from safety. His legs were feeling slightly rubbery. He kept sprinting. Forty yards. Another bomb blast lit up their faces again. He could see Murphy, and Fletcher, and the long face of Bristol. His fellow soldiers. His friends. His brothers. Thirty yards. His breath was coming hard, his lungs were burning, his heart pounding. Blackness. He kept running. Another flash of light and a sizzle went past him. Twenty yards. He was going to make it! Then, a man went flying through the air past him, thrown by the force of a bomb. Matt felt as if the whole world slowed to a snail's pace. Dark, light, a huge, thunderous explosion flung him forward. Matt saw the faces change from encouragement to horror, and as arms reached out for him, he saw them all being flung in different directions in a blinding flash of light. Then, nothing.

---

MATT WOKE UP SLOWLY, opening his eyes that felt dry and hot. He looked around and could tell that he was in a hospital near the front. He could still hear the big guns blasting in the background. He saw the canvas all around him and several rows of beds lined up with neat spaces in between. Most of the beds were full. He estimated there were about twenty-five beds in each row, giving the whole tent a capacity of around a hundred. He saw a few men from his unit that had been waiting for him at the edge of the woods nearby. One man was unconscious, another was awake and writing a letter, and a third lying with his head wrapped in bandages. He also had a sling around one shoulder.

Suddenly Matt realized his head hurt badly. He raised a hand to feel his head and felt a bandage. He tried to sit up and a feminine voice said, "Not yet, please."

As Matt turned toward the voice, he realized two things: It belonged to a small, beautiful nurse that looked too young to be where she was, and his leg felt as if it were on fire. His ankle also throbbed with a different kind of pain. His eyes traveled down to the ankle and saw more bandages. His leg was wrapped up to the knee. He raised his eyes questioningly to her face. It was pretty, heart-shaped with serious sea green eyes.

"You've a head injury. And your ankle is sprained badly, as well as burned. You have a small piece of flesh missing from your ankle, but the doctor was able to stitch it closed relatively easily. You mustn't move much until your head wound calms down. A doctor will be looking at you soon. My name is Sadie and I'm your nurse."

"Ma'am. Pleased to meet you. I am Lieutenant Matthew Smith. The fellows that were with me?"

Sadie nodded her head slightly. "They are here. If you could tell me their names, I will get their condition report for you." She was small but had an air of confidence about her that Matt had only seen in much older nurses. "My friend Minnie will be along shortly. I'm usually in the surgery, but they needed help in here today, so you are stuck with me." She smiled, and Matt felt as if the room got brighter. She was so pretty, and so different than the dirty, disheveled men he spent his days with on the battlefield. Her dark eyebrows matched the dark, curly hair that was barely contained under the nurses cap.

"Thank you, ma'am." Matt shifted uncomfortably. "I'd like to use the erm… necessary."

Sadie indicated the crutches leaning against the wall next to the bed. "Call me Sadie, or at the very least Nurse Sadie. It doesn't do to stand on formality under these circumstances. But don't tell Miss Frain that. She's our charge nurse. You can have an orderly help you to the necessary or try yourself. Mind your head wound."

Matt nodded slightly. It hurt.

After he was settled back into bed Sadie noticed he looked pale. She chatted with him while she changed his bandages. His head didn't look too bad, but the burns on his leg was enough to keep him here for a little while. She tried not to pay too much attention to how handsome he was and to concentrate on her duties. His well-shaped jawline and high cheekbones gave him the look of an aristocrat rather than a soldier, yet he was very masculine.

Matt watched her carefully as she explained to him that he had been thrown several yards and hit his head at the base of a tree, and that it could have killed him, so he was fortunate. She told him she would get him letter-writing materials if he wished and that she would check on him later. Then, his angel disappeared, and he didn't see her again until evening.

---

Sadie was taking a break in the meeting tent. She was sitting with Bridget and Minnie and talking about the latest group of soldiers that had come in.

"It certainly has been lively," remarked Bridget. Her eyes squinted slightly, and she looked pointedly at Sadie. "Your Lieutenant Smith is a handsome one."

Sadie flushed slightly and gave Bridget a sideways look. "He's not mine, silly. Yes, he is very handsome. I'm aware."

"At least we haven't lost anyone in a few days," Sadie sighed. "I'm glad for that at least."

Bridget nodded. "I must say, some of these poor boys just need some peace. I don't know if they'll ever be right again."

Minnie said, "Girls, we know that these men are wounded in spirit as well as body. We just do the best we can." She reached out and took Bridget and Sadie's hands. "I'm so grateful to be here with you, and Bertie."

Just then, Dr. Townsend came into the tent to get lunch. All the female eyes in the room found him. He was very nice-looking as well as pleasant. He had a bedside manner that Dr. Carter could have learned a lot from. He kept to himself, often, probably because he was just so tired. Sadie had never seen someone so young with such old eyes. Hilda would have said he had an old spirit. He sat by himself off to the side, glancing up just once and meeting Sadie's eyes. He smiled slightly, then went back to his meal. When he was finished eating, he immediately left the tent. Bridget looked at Sadie.

"My goodness, he is handsome!" she exclaimed. "Don't you think so, Sadie?"

Sadie chuckled drily, "Bridget, there is no time for that. It is against the rules so you might just as well forget about it." She thought of Matt, and a tiny group of butterflies stirred to life in her stomach.

Bertie was taking today off for a much-needed

break. She was spending a day picnicking with Red. Sadie was happy for her; Bertie deserved another chance at happiness. They all did. Sadie didn't know if anyone could see beyond this place, this awful war. She for one wouldn't be making any plans for the future.

Bridget flipped a lock of red hair back from her face. "Nurse Frain is a good nurse, but she does appear to be sucking on a lemon most of the time." The girls snickered at this.

"She takes the Army rules very seriously. No nonsense will be tolerated!" Sadie imitated Nurse Frain's stern tone perfectly. This made the girls laugh harder.

"We can be compassionate healers," said Bridget. "There's no need to be gloomy and glum. That's what the doctors are for. Imagine if we all had the bedside manner of Dr. Carter."

Sadie said without thinking, "I've just taken care of the most handsome man I've ever seen." Then she turned red to the roots of her hair. "I cannot believe I just said that." She was mortified. The butterflies suddenly felt like they had steel wings. She sighed heavily. What on earth was going on? She had never felt like this about a boy, or man, ever.

"It seems to me it's good that you even notice such things," said Minnie with a gleam in her eye. "We've all wondered why you never talk about a beau."

"Goodness, there's never been time!" Sadie exclaimed. Between the farm and spending so much time learning about healing from Hilda, then taking care of her father, and then nursing school, she had been way too busy to think about love. Now, she thought of the handsome Matthew Smith, and wondered.

11

MAY 27, 1918

Matt grunted with effort as he put weight on his injured ankle. The doctor had said not to do much walking yet, at least until the burns began to heal, but Matt was determined to get moving again. He walked a little bit every day as far as he could, but it was painful. There should be no lasting damage according to the doctor, however, it would take some time and patience. Additionally, burns needed to be mostly healed before they would allow the soldiers to return to battle.

He tried not to think about the pretty nurse, Sadie Prentiss. Truthfully, other than wondering how the boys back on the front were faring, it was hard to think of anything else. When she walked past, he sat up a little straighter in bed. Matt had never suffered from a lack of female attention, but he had always been preoccupied with work or the Army and hadn't taken much time for such things. He remembered a few girls from the lake back home, and how they flirted and giggled and were very silly. That seemed like a lifetime ago. Sadie didn't seem as if she had ever acted silly in her life.

Now, for the first time he could ever remember, he was interested. The timing was terrible. They were in the middle of a war, and it was strictly forbidden for a patient to be involved with a nurse. During his week of being in the hospital he had found out that several men in his unit had been killed. His first loyalty and obligation belonged to them. He needed to get well so he could return to the front.

He spent as much time as he could with the boys that were wounded battle with him. They played cards, chess, talked, and joked as much as they could. It was difficult because some of them were gravely injured. Matt was determined to make the time he spent here being useful and productive, if possible. He struggled for a few more steps, then went back to bed, for the time being. He could write a letter to his mother and to Henry while he was waiting for the next opportunity to get up. Letters sent back home were a bit simplistic due to the censorship of the Army.

They were careful not to write about the true

devastation of the war, nothing too truthful, in other words. The Army insisted on the boys keeping it light for the folks back home. He was sure that his mother and sister and the other folks back home made light of their circumstances as well. His Aunt Nettie, who was one of the tireless volunteers working with the Daughters of the American Revolution, was always sending cheery, news-filled letters from home. She kept him abreast of any news worth knowing, as well as sending encouragement in the form of home-baked cookies and candy and warm clothes that she and the other ladies worked tirelessly to produce for the boys overseas.

One day about a week after he had arrived at the hospital, Matt was walking slowly between the tents on the boarded walkway when he spotted Sadie sitting outside of the tent housing the gas victims. She was clearly struggling; her head was down, and she looked forlorn. He had seen firsthand how hard the nurses worked. They cared for their patients twenty-four hours a day. The nights were long, pain-filled misery for most of the soldiers, and the nurses gave medicine and comfort in equal measure. Since Matt didn't have excruciating pain, he was more aware than some of how hard the women worked. It was no easy feat to care for men with terrible injuries. Because some of them seemed so young to him, he was astounded at how strong and courageous they were. Seeing her quiet distress moved something in him.

---

SADIE SAT on a bench outside of the gas tent. She had just helped a young man write a final letter to be sent home to his mother. She'd had to write it for him as he had been blinded by the gas. She had been compassionate, kind, stoic, for the sake of the boy. He had been seventeen, a British boy. She had shoved down the disquiet in her soul as she had strained to hear him speak. His voice was raspy and was gasping for air and coughing up fluid. He had wanted her to write:

DEAREST MOTHER AND SISTERS,
    *I am taking a bit of a rest from the front. I have had an injury. I miss you all very much and would like very much to see you soon. Perhaps our cousins could come, and we could have a picnic. The country is pretty her, so many poppies in the fields; it is beautiful. Things are not so bad here, but I wish to be home before long. Tell Catherine and Elizabeth I shall show them my postcards when I return home.*
    *Your loving son,*
    *Marshall*

. . .

SADIE'S EYES had blurred with tears. No sooner had she finished the letter than he began coughing desperately. His lips were blue, and she knew it would not be long. She murmured comforting things to him, and when he gazed sightlessly in her direction and said, "Mother?" she'd said, "Yes, I'm here."

He breathed his last and Sadie, not able to speak, motioned a nearby orderly over. She pulled the sheet up over the dear boy's face and excused herself. The orderlies would take over from here. Only if a soldier passed away at night did the nurses need to remove and prepare the body.

She drew in a deep breath and wondered at how easy it was for her to breathe. What must it be like for these poor men to struggle to draw breath? How could men devise weapons such as this? Would any of them survive? Would the men be able to be normal ever again after suffering such things?

Suddenly, through her tears, she saw a pair of boots in the general vicinity of her feet. Her eyes travelled from the boots, up a long pair of uniform-clad legs, and up to the handsome face of Lieutenant Matt Smith. She blinked her tears away and quickly got to her feet.

"Ma'am. Please, stay seated. May I?" He gestured to the space beside her on the bench. She nodded, still not trusting herself to speak.

He sat down stiffly. She felt strength in his presence. They sat in silence for a few moments and then Sadie asked, "How are your burns and ankle coming along?"

"I'm doing well, ma'am, thank you. You look as if you've had an awful day." He didn't know what else to say. This was a brutal, terrible place. Enquiring about the weather or other mundane things didn't seem necessary.

Sadie looked up at him briefly. His hazel eyes were steady and concerned. She flushed a little from nerves. Goodness, of all things to fluster her! Nursing was not for the faint of heart, but one direct look from this man had her feeling nervous.

"I...that is...just now. I had to write a letter for a young man to his mother. It-it was sad. He was dying. He tried to spare her from the truth of it. He was gasping...for air...and he's..." her voice dropped to nearly a whisper, "he's gone now." Tears were rolling down her cheeks.

Matt didn't say anything. He slowly reached over and placed his large hand on top of her small one, and gently squeezed. He left it there for some time. They sat that way until they could trust themselves to speak. Sadie said, "I have a brother here somewhere. He is all I have in this world, and if I think of him lying there, dying, I wished I knew that someone would be there for him."

Matt nodded slightly. "I have a brother here too. His name is Henry. We have one sister too. She's at home in Michigan. I had hoped to run across Henry but haven't yet. It's strange how I have run across some boys from back home, but not him." He patted her hand and removed his. She felt a little bereft but understood it wasn't really proper for them to be sitting there that way. She could hear Miss Frain's voice in her head, "Remember, a nurse's reputation must be spotless. Nonsense will never be tolerated!"

She smiled a little at this. Matt looked at her, puzzled. She snickered a little then, because it seemed ridiculous to think it was improper of them to sit here with hands touching with all the things she had seen since she'd been here. She explained to Matt, and he smiled. Then his smile faded, and he said, "I have never met anyone like you. Perhaps, if we had met at a different place, at another time…I would have liked to court you, I'm sure." He shook his head slightly. "I can't imagine life after this war. I don't know if I'll even survive. A lot of the boys don't. And some that do, aren't ever right again. I can't do that to any woman. But, while I'm here, would you help me walk a little each day? I would just like the company."

Sadie smiled up at him. "Of course. It's my job to help you get well." She reached over and gently squeezed his hand. "Thank you. It is so nice to talk to someone besides my nurse friends. By the way, I am from Michigan too." She explained where her little town was, and they discovered that they had grown up only a couple of dozen miles away from each other. As she went to her quarters after supper that night, she had something different on her mind; not the usual patients' conditions and prayers for all of them, those thoughts were always there, of course. But this was something new; it seemed a little bit unfamiliar, and a little bit exciting.

12

JUNE 1918

Sadie continued with her work in the apothecary. She gathered herbs and roots and flowers and put them in bundles and hung them upside down to dry. She made tinctures and salves. They had to make as much as they could during the quiet times because when they got busy there was no time. She had some girls that were with the V.A.D., the Voluntary Aid Detachment help her with organizing and storing the jars and tins. She didn't allow them to label them; that she took care of herself, wanting to be absolutely sure that the correct dosage was written on each container. They used salves for burns and rashes, and tinctures for everything from fevers to digestive distress.

In the afternoons, she would walk with Matt. She told him about how she had come to know so much about plants, and how young she was when she started healing. She spoke with fondness of Hilda, her mentor and friend, and how she missed her. He began to understand why she said her brother was all she had in the world. He was fascinated by Sadie; attracted to her because she was beautiful and intelligent. He had never met anyone like her in the world. He enjoyed her company; at the same time, he felt guilty being away from his brothers-in-arms.

His burns were beginning to heal nicely, thanks to Sadie and her poultices. Although the burned area itched, it had not become infected. He had seen and smelled a lot of infection in the hospital. It was the single biggest obstacle to healing for most of the soldiers. Some of them came in not only with wounds, but with infections they'd had out on the front. Miserable conditions such as rain and cold combined to make trench foot a horribly common occurrence, and the rats that bred everywhere spread disease as well.

---

SADIE ENJOYED WALKING with Matt every day. The hospital had been noticeably quiet for a week or so, and everyone knew that it was just a matter of time before the next big influx of wounded. She was pleased with his progress yet felt sad that he would be going back to the front when he was healed. She didn't imagine any kind of future for the two of them. It was horrible timing, and it was a cruel joke that she had met someone who she could have dreamed of having a life with and not being able to. She knew the chances of him surviving the war weren't good. One evening they were walking and discussing the end of the war.

"I'll go back to Michigan, I'm sure." Matt said. "I've had enough of this Army life. My family has a farm, horses. I'm a fairly good rider, so maybe I'll train horses or something of that sort. Or sell automobiles," he said with a grin. "And how about you, Nurse Sadie? What will you do after this old war?"

Sadie said wistfully, "My family had a small farm. When my father died a couple of years ago, we managed to keep it going for a while. But it became too much, and when Johnny wanted to enlist, we decided to sell. Fortunately, Papa had some money put by, so we came out all right. I imagine I'll go back to Miller's Creek. I like healing. I'd like to go back. However, I will not make plans beyond this war. I can't envision anything after it. Beyond today, in fact. I simply can't."

Matt looked down at her and gently touched her cheek with the back of his hand. "Sadie, I know it wouldn't be fair to you to make plans for the future. But I need for you to know that if I did see a future with anyone, ever, it would be you." He pulled her up, right off her feet into his arms and kissed her. A thrill went through her. He set her back on her feet and took one of her hands.

"Nurse Prentiss!" A voice cut through her euphoria. Matt dropped her hand like it was a hot coal.

"At ease, soldier." It was Dr. Carter. He sounded exasperated. "I simply need a word with Miss Prentiss regarding one of her patients."

Relief flooded through her. With her face surely red as a beet, she walked over to Dr. Carter. She didn't dare look at Matt.

"Sir?" she managed.

"Young Will Hawkins, the young fellow with the bad abdominal injury? He is out of his head with fever. I don't expect him to live. I thought perhaps your presence would be comforting to him." His cool glance met hers. "You have a very calming effect on the patients. It is noted and appreciated." He briefly nodded at Matt and then turned to go. Matt walked back to Sadie's side.

Sadie felt a little warm. "We'd best get back," she said quietly. They walked back to camp with a little more space between them then there had been.

13

Sadie was awakened by a shout of, "Incoming wounded!" and leapt out of bed. She quickly dressed and went to meet the ambulances. To her horror and confusion, she was met with a sight she couldn't comprehend immediately. Civilians were being brought in on stretchers, being unloaded from the trucks, and more were coming via wagon, an orderly told her. Worst of all, a crying child around four years old was being carried by an orderly, who set him down gently and was trying to console him. Sadie ran to the little fellow, who was bleeding from a shallow cut from the top of his head. He was thin and dirty, like all the people Sadie could see. She grabbed him up, nodded briefly to the orderly and asked breathlessly, "What happened to these people?" He replied he wasn't sure and hurried back to the ambulances. She was looking around, trying to see if anyone was missing the little boy, but saw no one. She carried him to the meeting tent to assess his condition and to find someone who knew what was going on.

There were perhaps a hundred or so filthy, half-starved looking people in the tent already. Dr. Fielding and Dr. Carter were there, both looking as if they, too had been rudely awakened from sleep. Sadie approached Dr. Fielding cautiously, not wishing to startle her little patient. "What is going on, Doctor?"

"Miss Prentiss," Dr. Fielding said, "We have around a hundred civilians that were displaced by the Germans. They lived in a small village approximately fifty miles away. There were mostly old folks and children, as well as a few men returned wounded from the war. The Germans ran them out, didn't let them take so much as a blanket with them. They had no food, water, nothing except the clothes on their back. They had been walking for a few days, no food or shelter. It was too rainy to stay still for long at night. So, they were walking at night and got caught in No Man's Land. They were fired upon by both sides before anyone realized they were civilians. One of our battlefield stations sent word and our ambulances went to meet them. They are being triaged, you should bring him over there, see if anyone is missing him. Oh, and none of them speak English. Find Gisele, or Marie, please," he finished, referring to the two surgery nurses who spoke French.

Sadie rushed over to triage with the young boy. When she arrived in the tent the scene was as awful as anything she had ever seen. Old women and men were being looked at by nurses and doctors, young children were crying, silently mostly, as they looked too weak to be boisterous. It was heartbreaking. She set the boy down and began cleaning his head wound. She soon discovered it was very shallow cut and wouldn't need stitches. She couldn't find anything else wrong with him save he was filthy and half-starved. She found him a biscuit and some water and gave it to him. He devoured the biscuit so quickly she thought he would be sick. She handed him off to one of the volunteer girls and hurried over to the surgery. The civilians were French, and Sadie was in search of someone that could translate, so they might be able to find the boy's family.

One of the French-speaking nurses, Gisele, came to help, and Sadie found out that the boy's name was Jean, and his mother had gone missing. His grandmother had been with him, but he didn't see her anywhere. Gisele offered to take him in search of her. Sadie found the majority of the civilians were in the overflow tent. She helped find them bowls of water to wash with and clean clothes. They were being brought food by the orderlies and nurses who weren't busy caring for the wounded. Sadie couldn't find a lot of decent clothes, but what she could find she distributed to those whose clothes were in the worst condition. The events leading to their arrival had Sadie sick with anger and frustration. Who could turn old people and children out of their homes with nothing? The people had no choice; if they stayed, they would have been killed, so they set out across a war-ravaged countryside trying to find someplace where they could get help. They found nothing along the way, only deep shellholes, corpses of men and horses, and ugly barbed wire crisscrossing the landscape. Several of their number had been killed in the crossfire between the Allies and the Germans, some of the rest had been hurt. All of them were malnourished and weak.

The little boy had been reunited with his grandmother for the time being. It was heartening to see him throw his arms around the old woman and bury his face in her neck. While Sadie checked her pulse, to be sure she was unhurt, she could see that most of the people weren't hurt badly, just scrapes and bruises and many twisted ankles from all that walking in the hilly countryside in the dark. As she turned away from the boy and his grandmother to see where she was needed next, she saw an old man suddenly pitch over to the side and hit the ground like a stone. She rushed to his side and found he had died. How tragic that this old man had been robbed of the privilege of dying in his bed, perhaps in his sleep, as he no doubt deserved, instead of being marched out into the night and being forced to walk in brutal conditions only to reach safety and die.

Sadie felt a growing anger at the Germans for having no respect or honor toward the innocent. If this is how they treated non-soldiers, how would they treat prisoners they captured? Sadie feared for any of the Allied troops captured by the enemy. She recalled Hilda's stories of how the white soldiers had killed so many of the Indians, many times including women and children. They had set fire to their villages and run them off with nothing, just as the Germans were doing now. Sadie thought now that the Germans weren't really any different from the white men in Hilda's time had been. *Dear God,* she prayed, *end this war, before we all lose our humanity completely.*

---

As if things couldn't get any worse in the midst of a bloody, devastating war, the influenza began striking without warning. It may have come in with one of the wounded soldiers, or even one of the nurses or doctors who had taken a hard-earned day of leisure and visited one of the villages for a change of pace. There were a few tea shops here and there that were popular spots for a doctor or nurse to get a much-needed break from the monotony of sickness and death. Because of the nature of the dreadful flu, it was nearly impossible to contain. It had spread throughout the world in the past year. As the weather warmed, it had slowed some and everyone the world over had thought it on the decline, only for it to come raging back.

This particular strain of flu was no respecter of persons. It struck old and young indiscriminately. It wasn't only those in poor health or frail old age that succumbed to it, but the young and healthy as well. The soldiers began to fall ill. First it was those with the gas injuries, as their lungs began to fail. Then it was all of them, and it spread so quickly the staff was astounded. One day, there were two men that fell ill, and by three days later, about seventy percent of the men were sick, as well as half of the nurses. Dr. Fielding and Dr. Waverly were both down, as was the indomitable Nurse Frain. The overflow tent had been cleared and the influenza patients had been moved in. The staff was required to wear masks and gowns and hang a sheet between each bed, to slow the spread of the insidious disease. No one seemed to understand why some got sick and some did not, but they knew that keeping their faces covered and attempting to keep their hands exceptionally clean helped. It was challenging in any circumstance to keep the patients' wounds clean and the fight against infection was constant. The addition of having to keep their faces covered and the constant washing and cleaning of all the equipment, sheets, and clothing was adding an element that even the most resilient of the staff found trying.

Sadie and her friends were working fifteen hour shifts while they tried to maintain the cleanliness protocol and take care of the soldiers. Also, the nurses and doctors that were ill needed care as well, and all the volunteer girls were working as nurses as well, trying to keep up.

Sadie was giving the patients tea made from plantain, mullein and echinacea to help with the terrible chest congestion that went with this flu. She had shown the nurses how to mix the herbs and make the tea; now almost every nurse at the hospital knew how to make the tea and they gave it to the patients three times a day. For some, it helped tremendously, for others, a little, and still the patients were dying in alarming numbers. She was alarmed at how low they were on some herbs, decided they needed to go foraging for more.

She asked Bertie if she could go with her, as the Army did not like the nurses to go out by themselves.

They went one morning after breakfast, each taking a large canvas bag to put the plants in. They found mullein in the meadow and harvested handful after handful, being careful as always to only take one-third of available plants to ensure the future proliferation of the plant.

The echinacea flowers were just beginning to open, but the plant's leaves and roots were just as effective as the flowers, so they harvested those too. Echinacea, the purple and mauve colored coneflower, grew abundantly in the fields.

After they found as many plants as they could carry, they headed back to the hospital. It had only taken a couple of hours, so they went to the apothecary tent and began bundling them and hanging them upside down to dry. They would use some of the plants fresh because their supply was running low. When they had finished, they went to get some lunch, then it would be back to seeing patients.

The orderlies had set up another five tents that each would temporarily hold ten patients each. They had the nurses in a separate tent from the orderlies and doctors. The Army had been suffering shortages of doctors and nurses as well, so those who were well worked every possible waking hour to tend to their own as well as the soldiers.

Sadie was expecting that she might become ill, yet

day after day passed and she was still healthy. She came to believe that it was because of all the plant teas Hilda had given her over the years. Hilda had said the people she was raised with didn't get sick often because of the plant-rich diet they consumed. It was often diseases the white man brought that killed them. Sadie was convinced of the truth of this more than ever as one by one, the nurses fell sick. First, Bridget came down with a high fever, then Minnie. Bertie hadn't seemed to be sick at all yet; she said with a chuckle she didn't allow mean things into her body. They were all terribly worried when one of the favorite young volunteers, Mary, began bleeding from her nose and coughing up blood. They all knew this was the sign of death. Mary passed away within twelve hours of getting sick. This was so different than losing a soldier. There was no time for a funeral, for any that passed from this. They gathered the bodies and stacked them like a gruesome cord of firewood, waiting for time and opportunity to bury them. Sadie had heard that some places were burning the bodies. She felt a deep sadness that a life could pass without a funeral. Later they would have memorials for the fallen.

They cared for Minnie, Bridget, and Nurse Frain, and after about a week, the women were mostly recovered. Tragically, almost all the French villagers that had come in had gotten sick, and little Jean's grandmother died, leaving him alone in the world. And then, like a light in the darkness, came a miracle; his mother had been found wandering in the countryside, injured, but alive and lucid. She was reunited with her son, and Sadie breathed a sigh of relief that one small chapter of this war had a happy ending. The civilians would all be sent on to a relief compound run by the Army and the Red Cross until they could be settled somewhere again. Out of all of them that had come to the hospital, only thirty-one were left.

# 14

## JULY 1918

As the nurses and doctors tried to keep up with the sick and wounded, they became more and more weary. It felt as if it would never end, this sickness and war and death. The Army had a strict policy regarding mandatory hours off but since the outbreak of flu had happened, no one had been able to take many days off. The weather was not too bad although it was a rainier than normal summer.

When the girls finally had an afternoon to rest, they spent it in the overflow tent playing cards with Red and a few of the other orderlies. Red and Bertie were pretty much inseparable when they weren't working, and the girls took delight in seeing how happy Bertie was. Sadie had learned to play chess and was getting fairly good at it. She could beat Minnie occasionally, who had confessed to only being able to beat one of her brothers in the game. It was something different to do, and it passed the time well enough and took all of their minds off their patients for a small window of time.

That evening, Sadie asked Bertie the question that had been on all of the girls' mind. "So, Bertie, how is it with that young man of yours?"

Bertie giggled and said, "That Red is funny. He says he wants to marry me!" She giggled and her contagious laugh set the rest of them off.

Then Bridget said, "You are the funny one. Why is that funny? Wartime and peacetime are different; there's no promise of tomorrow. And it's not as if you are getting any younger."

Bertie picked up a hairbrush and threatened to throw it at Bridget. She thought better of it and decided to throw her nurses cap instead. It smacked Bridget right across the top of her fiery red hair and mussed it up. Bridget cackled with glee that she'd gotten a rise out of Bertie, who was always so good-natured.

"All right, I'm sorry," laughed Bridget. "You're a young, young lass. But seriously, why shouldn't you feel like you can get married. You're more than of age, and you know what you want, right?"

Minnie smiled slyly, "Well, I wouldn't waste a bit of time. I'd marry Red if I were you, Bertie. He's exactly right for you. And his friend Marty is quite a charming fellow too."

"Oh, is that so?" asked Bertie. "I believe I did hear that Marty thinks you are just about perfect. He thinks you're just tall enough." The girls all laughed at this, as it was obvious that the nearly six-foot tall Minnie was a perfect dancing partner size to the six-foot-four Marty.

The talked turned next to Bridget. Minnie said sweetly to Bridget, "And how is our Dr. Fielding doing, Bridget? Have you had lunch with him alone yet?"

"No, not yet," replied Bridget candidly. "We talked about it, but with the flu and everything, there just hasn't been time. We will, though, soon. I am thinking we should all go on a picnic next day we all get time off. And Sadie, how about your Lieutenant Smith?"

Sadie said quietly, "He is not mine. We can't get involved. I may never see him again. He's going back to the fight and we both agree that we can't…well, perhaps after the war…"

Bertie smiled brightly. "Sadie, you have to live, like Bridget said. There is no promise of tomorrow for any of us." But Sadie was quiet the rest of the evening.

Sadie had just said goodnight to the girls when she was called to come to the surgery tent. She quickly dressed back into her uniform and pinned up her hair and flew over to the surgery. She was met at the doorway by Dr. Fielding. He informed her that the men coming in were in poor condition. They had all manner of injuries and they were all critical. She could see around thirty men being brought in by the orderlies and they were in a bad way. She could see bandages dripping blood, poorly wrapped head wounds, bleeding wounds from legs. She was experienced enough to know by now that this group of men had come from further away than any other ever had to be in such condition. The makeshift bandages had been put on with the understanding that they would be tended to within an hour or so, but clearly, they had been on for at least a couple of days and now they would need immediate care.

---

Sadie met Roger's eyes as he bleakly surveyed the room filled with bleeding, moaning, screaming men. "Sir?" She reminded him of something he shared with her in the early days. "One patient at a time, remember?"

He nodded abruptly, then gestured her to follow him.

Inside the surgery was a mess. Sadie could see around thirty men being brought in and laid on various tables as well as on cots around the perimeter of the tent. Roger immediately began working on the first man, who was bleeding badly from a poorly bandaged stump on his right leg. Sadie assisted a new doctor that she hadn't formally met yet. He nodded at her and they continued to work on the young man with a rash of cuts on his face and a huge gash on his arm. It had been stitched but Sadie could see and smell that it was very infected. The doctor, a man Sadie had not seen before, was cutting the stitches away from the wound. Without looking up, he said, "I am Dr. Lewis. Your reputation precedes you, Miss Prentiss. You have been doing fine work here. I asked specifically for you tonight."

Sadie glanced up at him. "Thank you, sir, and please call me Sadie." She began cleaning the wound since Dr. Lewis had finished getting the poorly placed stitches out of the six-inch-long laceration. The wound was leaking blood and pus and the edges were very jagged. Whoever had sewn this poor boy up had tried their best but being out on the battlefield conditions were rudimentary at best.

After they had cleansed the wound, Dr. Lewis surprised her and asked her to close it. She nodded and got to work, as he moved on to the next man. She the wound stitched neatly shut with thirty stitches in no time. She loosely bandaged it and then looked around to see where she was needed next.

"Nurse!" called out Dr. Carter. She quickly went to

his side and could see that he was tending to a man with a badly infected amputated arm. "I have to clean this up, it's a mess. He's out for now but mind that he stays that way."

Sadie found the masks used to administer the chloroform and ether. She readied the droppers with the correct amount and stood by. The young patient was covered in bites from the body lice that infested the trenches where the soldiers spent most of their days. He was burning with fever that may have been from trench fever or the infected stump. Sadie watched with some horror that the amputation had been done very crudely and probably had been done in a hurry to save the boy's life. The boy was lucky to be alive even though he was in poor condition at the moment. Fortunately, Dr. Carter said it looked worse than it was, and he had it cleaned up and rebandaged in a few minutes.

There were many more soldiers with infections. The doctors and nurses worked to find the source of the infections. Most were attributed to dirty wounds and deplorable living conditions in the trenches. A few of the men needed surgery on their abdomens, and Sadie assisted Dr. Fielding with one of them.

The wounds were horrific, and Sadie did not see much hope for the poor boys. The weapons used were designed to inflict maximum damage to a human body, and they did. The dark-haired young man they were currently operating on was losing the battle. His injuries were just too severe. He died during the operation. Dr. Fielding exhaled loudly and moved on. There was barely time to clean their hands in between patients. Sadie saw three more bodies being taken out of the surgery. The orderlies picked up men who had been lying on the floor and gently put them on the hastily cleaned tables.

It went on all night. Surgery after surgery. Infection after infection. One would live, one would die. There was blood everywhere. Sadie's apron was soaked with blood. She had blood on her face and in her hair. When they finally finished repairing a wound on the last patient, Sadie was surprised to see it was light outside. There were two other nurses still there, as well as the doctors. Dr. Fielding's eyes met Sadie's, and he gave her a weary smile. "Well done, Sadie, as usual. Get some rest now, you look ready to drop."

"Yes, Roger. Thank you." Sadie went to clean up as best she could. She was starting to feel light-headed.

---

ROGER WAS NEVER so grateful for his staff as he was tonight. Sadie was remarkable, as were the other nurses that worked in the surgery. He had lost a doctor and several nurses and orderlies to the influenza, and he was devasted by their deaths. He felt selfish for thinking he was relieved that Bridget hadn't been one of those killed by the flu. There was truly no rhyme or reason for who lived and died. Sure, they all said their prayers and did their best, but really anyone could die at any time, and that was an unsettling thing for a doctor. God had in mind a certain timeline for them all. He wondered about how the war affected that timeline. Did God let men, women and children die before He planned? Or would that mean He wasn't omniscient? If He was all-knowing, did that mean He planned for their deaths in such a gruesome manner? Roger's head was spinning. He figured he had better get some rest before asking any more questions.

Sadie washed and donned another uniform, thinking that she didn't have the strength to undress and redress before her next shift. She was just going to eat something, then fall into bed to sleep until she had to be back on duty. While she walked to the mess tent, the images she had not processed while she was frenetically working began flashing through her mind. Blood everywhere, Dr. Fielding's haunted face as he lost a patient and had to move on. The young man with the mutilated amputation. Orderlies hauling out bodies. The men screaming. A wave of weakness and nausea passed over her and almost made her fall. She took a fortifying breath and kept going. As she neared the mess tent, she heard her name. She spun around and suddenly the ground rolled underneath her feet, there was a loud rushing sound in her ears, and she felt the blood drain out of her face. The last thing she saw was Matt running toward her with a look of concern, almost panic, on his handsome face.

15

Matt had been returning to the mess tent for the noon meal. He had spent the morning sorting bandages for the surgery. He was determined to be useful during his convalescence. He was still some distance from the tent when he saw Sadie walking slowly along the walkway, in the direction of the mess tent, but she looked unsteady. Bridget was approaching from another direction. She called out Sadie's name. Sadie quickly whirled around, and Matt saw her pale face at the same time he saw her legs give out. Instantly he broke into a run, forgetting his ankle. He sprinted toward her, leaping over a bench that was in his way, determined that she not hit the ground, or the boardwalk. He caught her just in time. As she fell unconscious, he picked her up and asked Bridget sharply,

"Where is her tent?" Bridget gestured for him to follow her and they went the short distance to the nurses' quarters. Matt strode inside, setting Sadie gently on her bed and asking Bridget to remove Sadie's shoes. "Make her comfortable. I'll fetch the doctor."

---

SADIE AWOKE IN THE NIGHT, feeling queasy. She was confused. There was a dim light from the lantern next to her bed, and she could see Bertie's concerned face sitting next to her. What seemed more important to Sadie was a tray with food on it on the table. She was famished.

"Yes, ma'am, you do need to eat." Bertie laughed, relieved. "You worked all night and half the morning and didn't eat a thing! No wonder you went toes up!"

Sadie sat up, embarrassed. "I've never fainted in my life. I have a very strong constitution."

Bertie smiled broadly, but her words were serious. "Even a strong constitution needs food and water, love." She handed Sadie the tray. Stew and bread had never looked as good. Sadie was so ravenous she began eating immediately.

"Oh, my goodness. This tastes just heavenly. I must be starving." They both giggled then.

"Well, just so you know, the doctor said you'll be

fine, but you must rest for a couple of days." Bertie sighed. "Goodness, we were worried about you. You've been sleeping for fourteen hours."

"Bertie! I'm sorry." Sadie was mortified. "You haven't been sitting here too long, have you?"

"Just the last couple of hours," replied Bertie matter-of-factly. "Bridget stayed until around eight. Then Minnie stayed until just past one. It's four o'clock now."

Sadie finished eating and suddenly noticed she was in her nightgown. "Matt," she said weakly. "He was there."

"Funny how you look down at your nightgown and think of Matt."

Sadie blushed furiously, but thinking Bertie wouldn't notice in the dim light, said defensively, "That's the last thing I remember was him running toward me-Oh! His ankle!"

"He did mess up that ankle just a bit, but the good news is that he caught you before you hit your head on the ground. Lord, he is handsome. He'll be all right. Bridget got you undressed. We have been taking turns bringing you food so that when you woke up it would still be hot."

"Which doctor…?" Sadie began.

"Dr. Carter." Bertie looked at Sadie questioningly. "I don't know how bad it was in there, but it's safe to say that Dr. Carter thinks the world of you. He said that you were as steady as any doctor he's ever seen. Now, please go back to sleep. Doctor's orders." Bertie gave her a quick hug and went to tell Bridget and Minnie. They had both taken a night shift so that Sadie wouldn't be disturbed. Then she returned and went to bed as well.

Sadie slept until noon. She was mildly embarrassed that her friends had undressed her. Silly, for a nurse to feel that way. She thought of Matt running to catch her and she felt warm all over. The chivalrous act may have delayed his healing. She thought that thanking him had better be the first thing she did today.

There was another tray of food next to the bed. She was still feeling famished, so the beef sandwich and canned fruit looked delicious. She visited the privy, then returned to bed and lay back down. Just like that, she was out and didn't wake up again until the next morning. Horrified that she had slept so long, she quickly dressed and went to the mess tent. There were only a handful of people inside. She spotted Minnie so she went over to sit by her.

"Minnie," she began quietly, "How could you let me sleep so long? I'm so embarrassed."

Minnie smiled her beautiful, gentle smile. "We were told not to disturb you. Between the extra work with the flu and that long night in the surgery, you have been through a lot. If it makes you feel better, some of the doctors slept for twenty-four hours after that night."

Sadie smiled a little. "Thank you, Minnie. For everything. Now, I need to find Nurse Frain, then Matt."

---

S{\sc adie went} in search of Nurse Frain and found her in the office. The brusque-mannered older woman looked kindly at Sadie and asked her to sit down. "My dear, you are a hard worker. You must learn when to take a break. The surgery is difficult for the doctors and orderlies, not to mention the nurses. I think most folks forget that you are just one girl. We are all so grateful for you. Please look after yourself. Dr. has suggested more sunshine and fluids for you, just as we prescribe the patients."

Sadie realized then that she hadn't been outside much during the day lately. There was always so much to do, and the influenza had made everything so much harder on everyone. She said, "Yes, ma'am. Thank you, ma'am."

"Today you can work straightening the apothecary and seeing what we are out of and see about procuring more herbs and so forth. There are some being held in

Paris at the main Red Cross hospital there. They were sent over with the last group of nurses and orderlies from back home and will be sent over here as soon as there is someone available to get them here. Since you have exhausted yourself," Miss Frain paused here to send a slightly condescending look at Sadie, then continued, "I believe it would be best for you to spend the next day or two overseeing the supplies, not just the apothecary, but the medicines, medical equipment, and bandages as well."

"Yes, ma'am." Sadie knew better than to argue. Truth be told, she was ready for a quiet day or two among the tinctures and salves, preferring the smell of plants to the smell of antiseptic and the other not so pleasant aspects of nursing.

She spent a pleasant afternoon in the small tent with the collection of jars and bottles. She was a little concerned that they were low on so many of the fever-reducing tinctures. They were so helpful when used in addition to aspirin with the patients. Too many aspirin caused bleeding problems, and there just wasn't a lot of choices to be had in treating the influenza and the infected wounds they saw so much of. She made careful notes of how much they had used in the past month, and recorded the numbers in two separate notebooks, one that remained in the apothecary and one for her personal records. She looked for some other herbs that were stored in jars on shelves along one side of the tent. The jars contained some dried plants that Sadie was familiar with, but some she wasn't as well. Also, there were some missing that she knew would help with wound healing that most white folks didn't use much but that Hilda had said the Indians used almost daily. In addition, she had brought her book and notes from home, even though she knew most of them by heart. One couldn't be too careful with plants.

She thought fondly of Hilda, and she could see her in her mind's eye, walking, slightly stooped with her old age, with her floppy-brimmed man's hat and her walking stick. They had walked so many times in the woods and meadows, especially in the autumn, when most of the herbs were ready to be gathered. Sadie looked forward to autumn every year. The smell of the freshly fallen oak leaves in the forest, the bright orange, coral, and crimson leaves of the sumac and sassafras, the lovely scents of the drying sage and other herbs as they filled the small cabin that where Hilda spent her nights in the fall and winter. She remembered watching the squirrels scurrying around, always busy gathering, digging, and burying acorns. They would twitch their tails and scold her if she got too close. She smiled at the thought. The smells and sights of autumn filled her with joy; it was her favorite time of year.

This fall would be like no other between the war and the influenza. When Christmas came this year, who knew if they would be in a warm place with friends and family, or still here in this brutal place full of pain and death and suffering. And to make everything worse, she had no idea where Johnny was. He could be dead or injured or alive and well. Not knowing was the hardest part. Added to that uncertainty was the randomness of death that the flu had brought. It left Sadie and her friends feeling as if the ground under their feet was no longer solid. She shook off the gloomy thoughts. The sun was out today, she would get some fresh air, and after supper, go find Matt. She had to thank him for coming to her rescue.

# 16

Sadie went in search of Matt after supper. She was afraid to see him in a way, embarrassed that she had been the cause of his delay in healing. She entered the tent and found him sitting up in bed, helping a friend with an arm in a sling write a letter home. He grinned when he saw her. She felt her face grow warm. His friend nodded and moved away so she and Matt could speak alone. Private wasn't the word, there were far too many patients and staff about for that.

"Nurse Sadie, you are looking a little better than I last saw you," Matt said with an innocent smile.

"Lieutenant." Sadie stood up as straight as her five-foot-one inch would allow her. "I don't—"

"Matt," he said. And winked at her!

Now she was tongue-tied as well as embarrassed.

"I'm only teasing, Sadie. Are you quite well?" Matt looked completely serious now. She nodded.

"Matt, truly, I am so grateful to you for being there. I don't know what would have happened if I had hit my head. But your ankle…" she broke off, feeling miserable.

"It is only a little bit sore, Sadie. Don't fret one bit about it. The burns were the main reason I was here so long, and those are still mostly healed. The ankle is just a little tender, it will be fine. I will more likely as not still be back on my way before long." His eyes captured hers for a moment. "I am glad I was there. I saw how white your face was, and when you started swaying, I knew what was coming. Everyone knew how rough those boys were that came in that night. You worked for somewhere around the entire night and half the morning. And it wasn't easy stuff. We've all heard stories." Sadie nodded.

"It was rough on the doctors too," Sadie said quietly. They lost more patients in that group than I've seen them lose before. It was just so sad. They were in deplorable condition. The boys had been caught in crossfire and trapped for a couple of days before they could get to the first aid station. By the time we got them, most of them had infections. We did everything we could, but still I think a third of them were too severely injured. By "the time we had finished, I was famished and all I could think about was getting food and going to bed. I was feeling woozy and when Bridget called my name and I spun around to see who it was, that made my head swim, and then, you know the rest".

Matt looked up at her and smiled. Lord, he was handsome.

"Nurse Sadie, it was my pleasure to catch you. My ankle is not so much the worse for wear. What kind of gentleman would I be if I had let you fall?" Then his eyes gleamed slightly wickedly, "You are a delightful armful I must say."

Sadie blushed to the roots of her hair. She couldn't speak for a moment.

"I'm sorry, Sadie. I don't mean to make you feel uncomfortable." She was getting lost in his eyes.

"Matt, truly, I apologize. I am truly grateful for you being there. And I am so sorry that you were hurt again."

Since Matt was getting restless being laid up, he said, "I believe I'd like to go for a walk. Would you be able to accompany me?"

His eyes were studying her face. Sadie began to wonder if he found her lacking somehow.

"You have the prettiest eyes," he said quietly. He stood and stepped closer to her.

"I'm finished working for today. Perhaps a short walk." She felt his presence acutely.

"I think a short walk is all I can manage," he said with a quick grin. "Shall we?" They walked around the entire camp, which was surprising to Sadie. She would not have thought he was up to that after his sprint to catch her, but he did a fair job walking. He let her take his arm and he used a cane to help, and they went slowly. She was not supposed to be alone with him, and especially at night. That was frowned upon by Miss Frain, but Sadie didn't care right at the moment.

---

MATT LOOKED DOWN at her and reached out and took her hand. He brought it slowly to his lips and kissed it. "Sadie," he began in a low voice, "I know I have no right to feeling this way. And I know that the Army forbids you to be romantically involved with a soldier. I have to go back to the front soon."

Without thinking Sadie slipped her arms around his neck and leaned toward him. He bent his head and kissed her, and her thoughts whirled. She was overcome with mixed emotions as the thought of finding him, finding this, and losing it again was almost too much to bear.

Matt groaned and said, "Sadie, I think I'm falling for you." He shook his head slightly and said, "If only we had met somewhere else, or after this. This war that has been going on for so long. I have never met anyone like you. You're so strong, and you're so kind, and...beautiful."

Sadie flushed. She was feeling too many things and trying to sort them out was very difficult being so near to him. She finally said, "I feel almost...cheated. To have met you here of all places and knowing that you must go back to the fight. I cannot allow myself to get close to anyone. I do not want to lose you. So, I think it's best if we don't...walk anymore." She pulled away from him and turned around. She had a lump in her throat from trying not to cry. Lord, was there ever be a time where heartache wasn't around every turn?

Then suddenly Matthew grasped her by the shoulder and turned her back to him. He lowered his head and kissed her gently. He took hold of both of her hands in his. "Sadie, I am almost healed enough to go back. I cannot ask you to wait. But, after this war, well, then things will be different. I am not going to give up on this." Sadie felt tears prick her eyes. Before she knew what was happening the tears were falling and he pulled her into his arms and held her while she sobbed. She cried for them, for the possibility of what could be or what could have been. She cried for all the young men who had perished so horribly and for their mothers and sisters and sweethearts back home.

After the storm had passed, he dried her face with his handkerchief. "All right, now?" he asked gruffly.

Sadie nodded, not trusting herself to speak. They walked back to camp in silence, both consumed with thoughts of elation and sadness, hearts bursting with joy and sorrow all at once. Sadie immediately went to the young man with the mop of blond hair who was in the throes of a fever. She spoke to him softly and held his hand. He settled down and was quiet, for the most part. After an hour, he was still.

# PART II

## 17

The war raged on. The armies on both sides were suffering. They were hungry, sick, filthy, and were growing despondent. After nearly four years of brutal fighting, the Germans had currently pushed the Allies back to the point where the constant booming of the huge guns could be heard at the hospital. There was a point when the nurses had to take cover in the emergency trench in the middle of the camp. They were rousted out of bed at 3 a.m. to the sound of huge blasts very close to the hospital. The girls rushed to the trench where they were holding on to each other for dear life when a comical sight appeared before them. Nurse Frain, in her nightdress, marched down into the trench with a porcelain washbowl held over her head like a helmet. They laughed despite the terror of the situation. They would all be sent to the trench for cover a few more times before the Allies pushed the Germans back far enough to where the hospital would not be so close to the actual fight.

---

## October 8, 1918

MATT WAS AWAKENED from a deep sleep during the night. There were few nights of good sleep with the sounds of a hospital at night and the sounds of the guns always there in the background. This particular night, however, the guns were quieter, further away, and the men in the ward were fairly quiet.

"Sir? An important message has come in for you." The young soldier hurried away. Matt quickly dressed and followed. There was another officer in the meeting tent waiting for him.

"Sir. Sergeant Blakely from the 23$^{rd}$ division near Paris. There is an officer and a few men up at Chateau-Thierry and they are trapped between two small German outfits that haven't stopped firing for days. We need a good rider to get to the boys of the 120$^{th}$ and get them out."

Matt pondered this for a moment. He was slated to go back to the front in two days. He was one of the best riders anywhere. He nodded. "Give me ten minutes." Then he went to quickly pack his things and have them sent on ahead of him. He would not be able to carry anything while he was riding.

He finished dressing and penned a note for Sadie.

*My dearest Sadie,*

*You are the most special girl I have ever had the privilege to know and spend time with, even here. I am very much smitten with you and would love to court you properly after this war is over. I have been summoned back and regret not being able to say goodbye in person. I will see you after this dreadful war, back in Michigan. If I cannot find you, here is my address:*

*Matthew Smith*
*37 Birch Lane*
*Clearview, Michigan*
*Until we meet again,*
*I am yours most truly,*
*Matthew Smith*

He tucked the note under his pillow, just a small corner of it sticking out. Sadie was usually there first thing in the morning and would find it. He hoped the note would give her comfort and hope for the future. He returned to the meeting tent and followed the young Blakely to the stable. He found the beautiful, powerful war horse he was to ride, and a thrill went through him. He got his directions from the sergeant and was off.

Sometime, in the early morning hours, Minnie came in and seeing almost all the beds were occupied, quickly gathered the sheets, blankets, and pillow from Matt's bed. She threw the pillow away as the highly contagious flu had made it impossible to clean them. She put the sheets and blanket in the dirty laundry basket, moved to the next empty bed and repeated the process.

---

MATT RODE as hard as he dared in the dark. Fortunately, the moon was almost full, which helped illuminate the trail. At daybreak he urged the powerful horse on, covering as much ground as was possible without tiring out his mount. Up hills, down narrow passes along creeks, jumping crevices and cracks here and there. Matt was enjoying being on horseback again after being cooped up in the hospital for so long. The horse was a black thoroughbred named Ares, and if Matt was not mistaken, he was also having the time of his life. His thoughts were on this ride, his mission. He would think of Sadie later, when it was safe. He rode, mile after mile, and sometime in the late morning he found the 120th. Or rather, a group of men that were in the 120th very unofficially. They were very well hidden; if he had not known where they were, he would have ridden on by. As he approached the camp, he called out the code word he had been given. A soldier appeared from behind a tree and met him. He led Ares away to tend him so Matt could get to business. The 120th had at their disposal a group of men that were hardened soldiers, guns for hire. Matt understood the need for such men in times like these. He reminded himself to remain vigilant around them, for they would do anything for money. They would go into a battle against the odds because they were paid well to do so.

Matt found a group of around thirty men sitting around looking fierce and ready to fight. Here were the hardest of men, the mercenaries, who killed the enemy without hesitation or mercy. They were hired killers; those who did things others would not. They were the sort of men needed to rescue the small group that was trapped between the two enemy lines. They had been awaiting their next mission, and Matt's message galvanized the men into action. Matt carried with him a rough estimate of where the officer and his men were as well as an idea of how many men it would take to get in and get them out.

By the time Matt had eaten a meal and rested a bit the mercenaries were ready with a plan. They had among their number a few snipers and explosive experts as well as men who had cavalry experience. A wiry, dark-skinned man asked Matt if he was joining them. He grinned. "Of course."

Other than knowing the rough location of where the soldiers were holed up in a rugged section of countryside, their rescuers did not know any details. They didn't know how far the stranded men were from each side, or how many Germans had them pinned down. What they did know was the country. This group of men were from all around the world. Among them were trackers, mountain men, goatherders, soldiers, scouts, and snipers. They even had an army medic among them, which came in handy, according to one of the men. Since he had an eye patch, Matt was assuming he knew what he was talking about. There were Turks, French, British, Canadians, and Americans, and they had been out here for three and a half years. The leader, a British fellow named Jack, knew this country like the back of his hand. He knew every trail, tree, and rock within a hundred miles. The fellow with the eye patch's name was Ricky and he looked tough enough to eat nails.

The kid that had taken care of Matt's horse was a speed rider. His job was to distract the enemy and he was so fast that he had never been hit. His horse was a sturdy little mustang. As they all mounted up, they readied themselves for yet another deadly mission. They knew what would happen if they were captured. They were not allowed the courtesies of most prisoners-of-war. They would be killed immediately. Someone, somewhere, had a list of the next of kin of the men. It was a short list as most of them had no family.

Along the way Matt learned that this group had carried out many of the same type of operations already. Matt was curious as to how a man became a soldier of fortune. It was definitely not for him. As they grew close to the trapped men, they dismounted. Four of the men stayed back with the horses to keep them at the ready. Then, with nothing but hand signals and the intuition that came with working together for so long, the group stealthily approached.

18

The Allies were slowly but surely pushing the Germans back. The news was good but the number of casualties coming in didn't slow. The fight kept on, the sound of the guns was growing more distant, but because of the flu, the hospitals were all short-staffed, so they kept bringing the soldiers to all the infirmaries, whether they were near the front line or slightly farther back. They brought the most severely wounded to the hospitals closest to the front line, so the injuries they were seeing at Field Hospital 5 were not bleeding out or showing up with mangled limbs, but they did get a lot of sick, whether from fever or the flu, and gas victims. The gas victims were always in various states of injury, depending on how much of the deadly stuff they had been exposed to or how long they had waited to receive treatment. There were still the men with cuts that needed re-stitching or wounds that needed irrigating. Worst of all, the flu was still making the rounds. It had died down for a few weeks and the staff had hoped that it was over. Then it came back just as bad as it had been, striking down the weakened soldiers and the tired, worn out hospital staff too.

All the hospitals on the front had sent urgent messages to Army headquarters, asking to send any available doctors and nurses to the front. They only got a few as there were the same issues everywhere. Sadie and Bertie were unpacking some boxes of supplies that the hospital had just received. Bertie was closely watching Sadie's face. "Love, have you been eating?"

"Yes, of course." Sadie said rather woodenly. She was quite pale, and her uniforms were too big on her. Food didn't taste good, and she ate, but apparently, she was losing a little weight anyway. She sighed. "Bertie, I'm not feeling the best. But it's not the flu."

"Honey, I know that. But you must try to keep up the faith. Your lieutenant may have had a very good reason to leave suddenly. An emergency." Bertie gave her a quick hug. "It will be all right, you'll see. Besides, if he does not have a good reason, there is something very wrong with him and you don't want him in that case."

Sadie smiled Despite her misery. Bertie was so

comforting to be around. She remembered going in to see Matt. His bed was occupied by someone else. She had been nervous about seeing him after their last encounter and her breakdown but had been excited nonetheless to spend a few minutes with him. She looked around the tent. Yes, this was Matt's bed. She saw Red and asked, "Red, where's Matt?" Her heart was in her throat.

"Lieutenant Smith left early this morning, around 4:00." Red turned bright red. "I know you were erm, friendly with him. I'm sorry." Sadie felt tears prick the back of her eyes. She nodded and choked out,

"Thank you, Red." She whirled around and strode out of the tent. She was devastated that Matt had left without saying goodbye. Did he kiss every girl he came across and leave without saying goodbye? That wasn't fair. It was war. He probably had gotten called away. She knew he was due to return to the front. She'd just thought she would have time to say goodbye. That was the trouble with handsome men. Always breaking hearts. She brushed a tear from her cheek. Enough of that, she thought. She needed to focus on her patients. That is what she was here for. It was probably for the best. But she really did not believe that.

ONE BY ONE, the nurses and doctors fell ill. What was different this time, no one knew. But of those who became ill, some had already been sick with it. Nurse Frain, Dr. Carter, and Bridget were all sick for the second time and in the influenza tent. Sadie had just finished lunch with Bertie and Red, and was getting her mask, that they were required to wear, tied on to her face when she heard a commotion coming from the tent. She hurried in to see several people gathered by one of the beds. Dr. Fielding was pulling a sheet up over a patient's face. She warily approached the group. A nurse turned and whispered to her, "It's Dr. Carter." Then she burst into tears and brushed past. Sadie felt rooted to the floor. Dr. Carter? That odd, stern, irascible man? She had grown fond of him. This did not seem right. How could the flu take down such a man? She felt as if the world under her feet was no longer solid.

## 19

Nurse Frain was still in bed with a ferocious cough. She appeared to be getting better, but Sadie did not take anything for granted anymore. She was applying a poultice to help with the cough when Miss Frain spoke in a raspy voice. "Sadie, my dear, you must eat more to keep up your strength and vitality."

"Ma'am, you should be concentrating on getting well and not worrying about me. I am fine. I am eating, I promise." Sadie finished up and smiled at the older woman. She was a dear underneath the crusty exterior. "I have been working long hours, as everyone has. I will try to eat a little extra." She went on the check on Bridget, who was the most cheerful sick person Sadie had ever seen.

As time went on, the second wave of flu passed, and they all hoped it was behind them. After a particularly long day, Sadie was washed up and ready for bed when Bertie came in with some mail for her. One letter was from Sadie's nursing school friend, Maude Beckett. The familiar name cheered her. Then she saw the other letter. It was a very formal looking letter from the Army.

"No, no, no," she whispered, feeling her knees give way. "The war is almost over." She began to gasp for air. Bertie rushed to her side and helped her sit on the bed. She sat down beside her and put her arm around Sadie while she opened the letter and stared at it disbelievingly, and she stayed with her for an hour after she collapsed on the bed, sobbing.

The news of her brother's death was the last straw for Sadie and grew despondent. She was the same with her patients, healing, comforting, caring, but after she had her meals, she spent more time alone than with her friends. She wondered around the edges of the camp, towards the woods, foraging, thinking of Hilda, Matt, and Johnny. In the back of her mind, she had known this was a possibility, but she had always thought he would make it somehow. Had she not prayed hard enough? Was he alone when he died? Misery rose inside of her. She was truly alone in this world now. She stuffed the feeling down. She had patients to care for. She could feel sorry for herself later.

As the weeks passed, she was becoming aware that the war was almost over. There was word that there was an armistice in the works, although no one knew for sure. They would keep on as they had, caring for patients, and hoping for the end of the war.

Time did not stand still for broken hearts. Sadie was thrilled one day at lunch when Bertie and Red announced they would be getting married soon. Minnie and Bridget were there too, enjoying a few minutes to catch up.

"We don't need a big wedding," chuckled Bertie. "We will have the chaplain marry us right here. And you will be our witnesses."

"Congratulations! Oh, what good news!" squealed Bridget. She, Minnie, and Sadie were delighted.

It was so uplifting to have good news to celebrate. Levity, happiness, smiling faces were all so rare these days. Everyone was worn out. They were all surprised by the news that the Army was holding a dance for the staff in the meeting tent. Everyone had missed out on their days off after the flu outbreak, so they were going to have a social event to boost everyone's spirits. Sadie was looking through her small drawer of belongings wondering what dress she would wear when she heard a sniffle. She looked up and Bridget was standing there holding a letter identical to the one Sadie had received just a few weeks before.

"Sadie?"

Sadie went to Bridget and exclaimed softly, "What is it?"

"It's my finance. He is dead. I-I sort of knew that he was gone a while ago. I just knew. But now, I know for sure."

Sadie reached out and hugged Bridget tightly. After a few tears, Bridget stood up straight. "Well, now that I know, I can carry on." With a quick nod, she said, "How about we go visit Miss Frain?" With that, they went to see how their charge nurse was faring. Miss Frain was on the mend, thank goodness.

Dr. Fielding was just finishing his rounds when he saw Bridget and Sadie come in to see Miss Frain. He approached them with a serious look on his handsome face. His green eyes were earnest as they rested on the girls. "Hello, Sadie, Bridget. I am so sorry about your fiancé, Bridget." Word traveled quickly, as it does, and everyone had seen those letters from the Army and knew what they meant. He had expressed his condolences to Sadie when she received that letter a couple of weeks before.

"Thank you, Roger," replied Bridget steadily. "I have felt it for a long time; this just confirmed it." She tentatively smiled at him. "Are you finished here? We were going to play cards after we see Miss Frain. Would you like to join us?"

"Yes. For just a little while," said Roger. "I'm in charge of gathering musicians for the dance, so I have some more work to do this week. I hope you ladies will be attending?"

"Most assuredly!" responded Sadie. "I think it is going to be very refreshing to relax for an evening. And music! I've missed it." In the midst of all the loss, something to look forward to seemed very much in order.

Bridget nodded in agreement. "I will be happy to get my mind off from things for a night. It is so very trying these days, getting through each day, hoping and thinking that the war will be over any day makes every day seem longer."

---

THAT EVENING when they were all getting ready for bed, Bertie said, "I think it will be good to have a social event here. We definitely need to get our minds off from all the tragedies, for a couple of hours anyway." She looked at the girls with a mischievous look. "Did you girls pack a fancy dress?" They all laughed at this, because they hadn't taken much with them at all when they came over here. They had brought a couple of dresses because they knew they would be supplied with uniforms, nothing too fancy, but they each had something that would work for an off-duty occasion. The truth was the idea of putting everyday dresses on would seem like a luxury when they had worn nothing but uniforms for so long.

# 20

Even though everyone was experiencing the heartache of loss during this time, everyone in the camp was looking forward to the supper and dance. It was going to be on Saturday of this week, the last week of October. There was word going around that the Allies had the Germans on the run, and that an Armistice was getting ready to be signed. The air around the hospital grounds grew different; upbeat, even the patients, the ones who were not too badly injured were smiling and joking. It was truly the best Sadie had felt about anything since the war had begun. It had been so difficult knowing that her beloved Johnny was gone and wondering what, if any, future she had after this war without him.

Bridget and Dr. Fielding exchanged interesting

glances fairly often and Sadie was quite amused by it. Roger was friendly to all of the nurses, impeccably mannered and courteous at all times, so when Sadie teased Bridget about the dance, Bridget flushed and said, "Look who's talking! I for one think Roger is taken with you, Sadie."

Sadie frowned at this. "Roger? Heavens, no!" She was slightly aghast at the thought. It was difficult to think of any man in that regard after Matt had left so suddenly. She would not be in a hurry to repeat the behavior that led to such heartache.

Bridget giggled. "I hope you don't have designs on him. I do rather like him. I hope he asks me to dance."

"Of course, he will, Bridget. Why wouldn't he?" Sadie was amused because they sounded as if they were thirteen years old. It sure felt good to speak of something besides irrigating wounds, amputations, and gas victims. They had a chance to have a good time, celebrate Bertie and Red's engagement, and it looked like the end of the war as well. It was a good feeling.

---

THE EVENING of the dance finally came. It was a nice cool night, not raining for once as it had been exceptionally rainy lately. The girls were glad that they would not have to traipse through mud anywhere for a night. It was a quiet time in the hospital, for most of the patients had been transferred out to Paris or sent back their home countries for their continued convalescence. There had been news that some of the field hospitals were packing up and moving out.

Sadie was finishing dressing and Bridget was fussing with her hair. Both girls had left their hair down, and Bridget was fascinated with how long Sadie's hair was when it was down. Her mouth fell open with astonishment. "I don't think I've ever seen your hair down, Sadie. It's marvelous!"

Sadie raised an eyebrow. "Really," she said drily. "I'm thinking of cutting it short, like a boy. I'm tired of it." That was an understatement. In truth, she had become so used to it that she probably would feel like a shorn sheep without it. She fluffed it out a bit with the toothed comb made from a tortoise shell that Hilda have given her years before. She smiled whenever she touched it. It was a pleasant memory from a difficult time in her life, when her hair had begun thickening up and making it impossible to tame.

Sadie's dress was green, which looked lovely with her sea-green eyes and dark hair, and Bridget's was blue, which made her cornflower blue eyes stand out even more. Her fiery red hair was halfway down her back and was fastened up on one side with a pearl hair clasp.

Minnie looked tall and slender and lovely in her rose-colored dress, and she had her hair pulled back on the sides and loose down the back. Bertie wore a navy-blue dress and was the only one who kept her hair up as usual, with her endless black braid wrapped around her head.

The girls all crowded around the small mirror in the tent and giggled with excitement. They felt young and giddy and happy for the first time since they had arrived in France.

They entered the meeting tent and were astonished at the sight. Instead of the plain old tent, there were flowers in large glasses all around, and the table was set neatly for a sit-down dinner. The normal method of eating was a hurried affair, eat your rations and get back to work. They were all seated with placards as if at a wedding, and were served a very extravagant meal; ham, corn, beans, biscuits, potatoes, and three types of pie. The girls were joking that they wouldn't be able to dance if they ate everything, but they ate everything anyway. It was so nice to enjoy delicious food, have a good conversation with someone and not feel that the world was ending. All the military doctors, orderlies, and nurses wore their dress uniforms, and Roger, being a civilian doctor, wore a nice suit and looked as handsome as ever. Looking around, Sadie thought they all looked a little thinner, but surprisingly good otherwise.

After dinner, the tables and chairs were cleared away, and a small parade of men came into the tent with musical instruments. One fellow had a banjo, one a harmonica, a few had brass instruments, and one a fiddle. When the music started, the nurses were all inundated with requests to dance.

Minnie was spirited away by Red's tall friend and looked to be having the time of her life. She was comfortable around men having been raised with so many brothers. She took everything in stride and didn't mind being teased. The other girls knew from experience that just because she was quiet did not mean Minnie was meek.

Dr. Townsend, whose given name was William, asked Sadie to dance, and she accepted. They didn't speak much, and since she had learned that he was shy, she was fine with that. She didn't feel much like talking much these days. She found herself smiling more as the evening progressed. She knew life would go on; whether she chose to be miserable or joyful was up to her.

Sadie was pleased to see that Bridget was dancing with Roger. They seemed to be floating around the floor as if they were in the grandest ballroom. Sadie was dancing with a nice young orderly with jet black hair and brown eyes. He was very charming, and she was having a great time. It felt so good to be dancing.

She wasn't the greatest dancer, but she did pretty well. She wondered if Matt had danced with a lot of girls. Where had that thought come from? That was not productive thinking at all. She was determined to forget him. She smiled up at the young man, whose name was Joe Briscoll. She was really having a nice time, feeling twirled around the floor felt so good. She danced with many young men, and then Dr. Waverly. He was so much fun; he had her laughing as he whirled her around and made jokes at everyone's expense. He was a good doctor, and he had a very winsome personality as well.

After a couple of hours, everyone was getting tired. The girls went for short walks outside to get some fresh air and rested on the benches that were everywhere. A few couples strolled here and there, not wandering too far, most of them anyway. It seemed so different to be outside at night, in a normal dress. Some of the more mobile patients had come out to smoke and talk to the doctors and nurses. They were chatting and laughing and having a good time too.

After a while, Roger spied Sadie sitting outside taking a rest. He approached her and asked if he could join her. She nodded and he sat down a respectful distance away. "Sadie, now that the war is almost over, I wonder if I could ask you something."

Sadie looked at him sideways. She did not feel that way toward him. Oh no. What would she say to him?

"Of course." Goodness, what was she to do?

"I, erm, well, it's just…I think I'm in love with Bridget." He looked slightly pained.

"What!?" Sadie stared at him. "Why on earth are you not out here with Bridget, then?"

Roger sighed. "I know that her fiancé is dead. She has only just found out. I do not want to rush her into anything, and I don't know how she thinks of me, or if she does at all. I…wondered if you have an opinion about whether she might, perhaps consider allowing me to court her?"

Sadie couldn't help it. She smiled broadly. "Roger, have you not seen the way she looks at you? Why, I have caught her many times stealing a glance your way! I don't think her fiancé has been on her mind much for quite some time."

He smiled rather boyishly, and Sadie noted again how handsome he really was. They made small talk for a little while, then they talked about Matt. Roger said, "I can't imagine why he would leave without a word, unless it was in a huge hurry. He may have had such urgent orders he had to leave in the middle of the night. I know we are all not supposed to get involved with each other here, but let's face it. People are drawn to each other. I'm sure he was taken with you. Do not give up. I don't think you've heard the last from him."

Sadie was quiet for a long moment, then she said, "Thank you, Roger. I have not allowed myself to think of him too much just because my job comes first right now. If he survives this, I might try to find him someday. I do not know if I'll be able to. He told me where he is from and I know I told him where I am from, so it just remains to be seen whether I am bold enough to go searching for him after he left here without a word."

Roger nodded. "I understand. Just remember that he did not have any reason to be untruthful with you. I think he cared for you. I can understand why he does. If it wasn't for Bridget, well, I just might have eyes for you myself. You are a remarkable woman, and the best surgery nurse I've ever seen." Sadie looked at him with a raised eyebrow. She chuckled.

"Well then, Roger," she said smoothly, "If things do not work out with Bridget, come and see me." She turned away, laughing, and headed back to the dance.

Sadie danced a little while longer. Then, the evening wound down and the girls, except Bertie, went back to their quarters to get ready for bed. They had fits of giggles with the stories of some of the men they had danced with, and Minnie said she was going to be seeing Red's friend again, after the war. Seeing her beautiful smile made Sadie feel happy and quite content. They were all just getting ready to go to sleep a couple of hours later when Bertie came in. They all looked at her and burst into peals of laughter.

"What is so funny?" demanded Bertie.

Bridget replied through her laughter, "Look in the mirror!" Bertie bent and peeked into the small mirror. Her hair was about halfway out of her tightly woven braid. She looked as if she had been up to mischief.

"I am thirty years old. Stuff it! You'd think a woman's hair didn't get a little messy while she was dancing."

"Yes, dancing," snickered Sadie. She threw a pillow at Bertie.

They all laughed harder, and Bertie joined in. It had been an eventful evening.

## 21

### NOVEMBER 20, 1918

The news was spreading like wildfire. An armistice had been signed! The war should be over, except that the hospital was still getting freshly injured soldiers. The came in far fewer numbers, after the first part of November, but skirmishes were still being fought out in the rough country where the soldiers had not received orders to stop yet, and they refused to give up. Finally, the order came to ceasefire. The staff at the hospital rejoiced. They learned that they would be packing up their hospital either at the end of January or beginning of February.

It had been rainy and cold the last couple of months, and now winter was settling in. Sadie and the other girls had to wear thick gloves and hats every time they left their quarters to report for duty. They had a small wood burning stove in their tent, but it grew cold by morning and they awoke to frigid temperatures and red noses every morning. The patient tents had been combined from four into one, since they were leaving soon and there were not many patients left.

Sadie was tickled to see that Dr. Fielding and Bridget had been spending time together since the dance. Bridget had a smile on her face more often than not. With Roger, it was hard to tell because he smiled frequently anyway. He seemed to be happy most always.

Minnie and the young man she had danced with all evening at the social in October were also courting. It was a bit easier now that the war was over officially, although everyone was still careful around Miss Frain. It would not do to get her all upset.

The fighting was dying down, slowly but surely; however, the hospital was coping with another wave of influenza, and it was spreading like wildfire. One day it was two soldiers, by the next day ten, then the next day there were twenty-five. Some got sick, and within a week got well again. Some got sick quickly and died by the end of the day. It was discouraging to know that the war was over, but the hospital was bustling with activity. This latest wave of sickness was more deadly than the previous one had been. Then the nurses began to fall sick again. Sadie was heartsick at how sudden the patients died. This time around, they lost fourteen nurses. They had sent for reinforcements around the middle of November, and around twenty fresh nurses and two new doctors arrived.

---

AFTER BREAKFAST ONE MORNING, just after Thanksgiving, Sadie and Bridget were getting gowned up for the surgery tent when they heard a loud commotion coming from the edge of the camp. A truck came roaring into the triage area, and the orderlies were running to meet it. It had been Dr. Fielding's turn out at the front line, and Bridget went white as a ghost when she saw him lying on a stretcher being carried toward the surgery.

Dr. Carter was there immediately, assessing Roger's condition and barking orders to the surgical staff as they hurried along behind him. Sadie and Bridget were on duty so they were informed that Roger had been hit by some shrapnel from an artillery shell that had exploded above the medical station at the front. He was bloodied but hadn't been mortally wounded. Bridget and Sadie assisted Dr. Carter in removing tiny shards of metal from Roger's face, neck, and arms. He would have some small scars, but he wouldn't be disfigured the way so many of the men had been.

Later that day, Sadie went to visit Roger. He was sitting up in the bed, with four large bandages on his arms and a few small ones on his face and neck. His eyes were glassy from the pain medicine and he was slightly pale. He had that look that all the wounded men had, stunned and sick. Sadie sat down beside the bed and patted his hand. "How are you doing, Doctor Fielding?"

Roger shook his head slightly and said, "I don't know what happened. I was patching up a fellow who was bleeding badly, and the medic next to me just... dropped. He was gone. He never knew what hit him. The other men, including myself, were all struck with debris, shrapnel, dirt, rocks. The noise...it was so loud, louder than it has been ever before. The Germans seem to be hitting us harder than ever. I don't think they know there's been an armistice signed. Either that or they just don't care."

Sadie explained to him that she and Bridget had helped Dr. Carter in the surgery and that Bridget was doing well even though it had been a shock to her to see Roger on a stretcher. "She's resting now, and she'll be in to see you this evening."

"Thank you, Sadie. You are a godsend, as is Bridget. I'd like to sleep now."

Sadie left him and went to supper. She was disturbed by Roger's accounting of what had happened. She felt that they were in danger just being this close to the fighting but had never imagined something like what he had described happening. He must be in shock. Roger and the other doctors and nurses had come to mean so much to her. She didn't want to lose anyone else. This war had to stop surely, since the armistice had been signed. Didn't that mean it was over? She wondered how much longer they could all hold on.

---

SINCE IT LOOKED as if they would still be here for Christmas, the Red Cross had sent some decorations and special items for a Christmas dinner. No one was feeling up to a party, but everyone was willing to try to help boost morale for the exhausted soldiers.

Some unexpected goodies had come from back in the United States. The ladies of the D.A.R., the Daughters of the American Revolution, had sent dozens of boxes of cookies, homemade candy, and knit items such as mittens, scarves, and hats for the soldiers as well as the staff. The D.A.R. was always sending things out to the front; blankets, and clothing items to help keep the freezing cold at bay.

Sadie, Bridget, Minnie, and Bertie were sorting out some of the treats so that all of the soldiers would have some. They kept some aside for the fellows who were too ill at the time to have them. Sadie hoped this would indeed help the patients feel encouraged, knowing that so many people back in the States were thinking of them. There was a huge bag of mail, and all of the girls were excited to have received Christmas cards and letters from loved ones.

Sadie got a letter from Maude as well as one from…Johnny. It was two months old. He must have written it shortly before he died. Johnny was doing all right for now, he said. He was "always cold" but doing the best he could under the circumstances. Sadie got a chill reading this precious letter from her brother. She could see a few smudges that could have been dirt, or something else. She wiped tears away as she put the letter in her suitcase with the other letters she had received over the last few months. Bertie got a letter from one of her sisters, Benjamina, and they all giggled again at Bertie's mother's taste in girl's names. Minnie got some letters from a couple of her brothers. At night, the girls would read to each other their letters and it felt almost as if they knew each other's families.

Thankfully, no one else had been killed, although the news in the letters was almost always a month old.

After a very hearty Christmas dinner the staff and soldiers sang Christmas carols, the ones who were able, and Sadie was moved to tears to hear the soldiers singing, "Silent Night." She thought of Johnny, and Matt, and her chest felt tight with sadness.

22

---

Sadie and Bridget were sitting on a box of supplies that was about to be loaded up into the trucks. They had been packing up for the last week and were supposed to be leaving soon. Roger had recovered from the flu, and although he had been somewhat weak and tired for a couple of weeks, he looked well. He came sauntering up to them, his green eyes alight with happiness. He paused behind the crate the girls were sitting on and said, "How are you ladies feeling about heading home?"

Bridget smiled, "I am so ready to be going, I could fly out of here!"

Sadie chuckled, "I can't wait to have a good hot bath and a long sleep. But right now, I think I will go check to see that I have everything ready. Bridget, do you have your bag?"

Bridget shook her head. "It's all packed but I just need to grab it. I thought maybe a short walk first."

---

SADIE FINISHED PINNING up her hair and placed her wooden box of pins into the small suitcase. The small box had a flower carved into the top and had been a gift from her brother for Christmas one year. She ran her finger over the intricate flower on the lid and smiled. Johnny had only been twelve, and she ten. She had always loved it. Now more than ever she treasured it.

The camp was moving out. She would be back on a train in a few hours and would be spending a few days in Paris and then traveling on to Bridget's homeland for a visit with her family. Sadie grinned to herself imagining a whole family people with red hair and freckles. She exited the tent for the last time and watched as a couple of transport men from the Army packed the tent up. They made quick work of it, and they packed it away in one of the biggest trucks. The staff would ride in the smaller vehicles, and even though it was not the smoothest ride, they all looked forward to it because it meant they were heading home. The men from transport had come specifically to help them tear the hospital down and escort them back to Paris; it looked to Sadie like there were about twenty of them. She was glad to have them for the extra protection. The roads were not exactly safe just yet, even though the war was officially over there had been skirmishes here and there and the doctors and nurses were not exactly prepared for combat. They were not expecting any trouble, but they needed to be prepared in case.

As they were beginning to get in the trucks, a man on a sweat-lathered horse suddenly appeared coming down the road from the direction in which they would be going. He skidded the horse to a stop and leapt off, falling to the ground. He was half-soaked in blood, and Roger immediately ran to the man. Sadie and Bertie followed, then the rest of them. From the looks of his uniform, he was a British soldier.

Roger ran out to the man, "Good God, man, what happened?" Sadie ran to find a medical bag.

"Guns!" the man croaked out weakly. "Get guns, now!" He looked around wildly. "Men raiding, killing everyone. They are out of their minds and not to be reasoned with. Please, they killed my friends. We were the last company across the river near Amiens, and they came out of the woods. They are on foot and they have guns. They are killing everyone. Said they are starving, to hell with us. My whole company is gone."

The doctors and nurses exchanged puzzled glances. "Soldiers?"

"Civilians…" the man was as pale as death. "Get your guns!" Roger gestured for everyone to go and they ran toward the trucks containing the weapons. They had some of them stored in crates in the back of one of the big trucks.

Sadie and Roger began trying to stop the bleeding. Roger was trying to get the man on his feet to assist him to one of the vehicles. They had just gotten him up and Roger grunted. He fell to the ground. Sadie shouted, "Help!" and stayed as low as she could, helping the man to the truck. Red and another orderly ran and picked Roger up and hauled him to a truck and put him in the back, then ran to get guns. Sadie, after helping the man up to the truck, turned and what she saw made her blood run cold. Around thirty men, dressed in ragged clothing and unkept in appearance were advancing rapidly toward them, in a line from the woods to the road, both blocking their exit and coming toward them at the same time.

Sadie leapt into action and screamed for Bridget to come with her. She ran to the truck where one of the orderlies was grabbing the guns and passing them out. He yelled, "Can you shoot?" Sadie nodded, and he tossed a gun her way. She caught it with both hands and turned immediately and took aim. The men were around twenty-five yards away, and Sadie could see that they were barely human. What on earth had happened to these poor souls that turned them into this?

They were dirty and blood-spattered and skeletal looking. Their eyes were wild, and they were muttering and yelling among themselves while they locked on the nurses and doctors that were facing them down. Bridget and Sadie both cocked their guns. Bertie was in the back of the truck with Red, getting more guns and checking that they were loaded. Minnie was out of sight at the moment.

Sadie's eyes met those of one of the scavengers. He bared his teeth and raised his gun. She fired, dropping him to the ground. She had been raised in the country without a mother and had learned to handle guns at a very young age. It had been necessary for her to help hunt and fish as well as scare away predators.

She saw another man carrying a blood-stained axe and he was raising his arm to throw it. A shot rang out, and he fell. Sadie saw out of the corner of her eye that one of the doctors had fired that shot. Another shot rang out, and another. Sadie fired again at a man that was running, toward the nearest truck. She hit him and he spun around and fell. The men kept coming, and

Sadie was horrified to see more men coming out of the woods. She kept firing as the men continued to stagger toward them. Clearly, they were weak from hunger, but something was driving them forward; an instinct to survive no matter what they had to do. One after another, they fell.

As soon as the first group of men was down, Red yelled for everyone to get in the trucks. They ran toward their vehicles, scrambled aboard and the trucks began moving out. The soldiers, who were in the back of each truck, shot at the stragglers and the men coming from the woods.

Sadie and Bridget collapsed into the back of the supply truck they had clambered into. Sadie became aware of a burning in her arm. Bridget's face looked white and pinched. She leaned toward Sadie. "Sadie? You're bleeding!" Sadie looked down and her dress sleeve was torn and there was a spreading spot of blood on it. Suddenly, she felt a little faint. Bridget helped her to lie down, then grabbed some gauze pads and held them against Sadie's arm.

Sadie looked at her arm, shooing Bridget back. "I'm okay. It's not too bad." It looked as if she had just been nicked by a bullet. Fortunately, it was not a serious wound.

Bridget sighed. After she, too, examined Sadie's arm, she said, "I do not believe you'll need stitches, but it should be properly cleaned as soon as we stop. There are only limited supplies in here and we most likely won't be stopping for a good while. At least until we know it's safe."

A young medic with curly dark hair and coffee-brown eyes crouched down in front of Sadie. "Fine shooting, ma'am," he said seriously. "You're white as a sheet, you should lie down."

Numbly, Sadie obeyed.

---

THE POOR FELLOW who had rode into the camp warning them was lying on the floor of the truck, where an orderly and doctor were trying to make him comfortable. "Roger?" she asked them, fighting for control of her emotions.

"He's in another truck, ma'am, I'm not sure of his condition. Dr. Harris is there too, looking after him," replied one of the soldiers.

"What on earth was that?" Sadie asked, not really speaking to anyone. She was shaking and sweating despite the cold temperature.

The man who had brought the message just in time to them was shivering, and Sadie could see that he was still bleeding profusely. She felt terribly sad, knowing this man had saved all their lives and probably wouldn't live long enough for them to thank him. She went to him to try to help, however, the doctor shook his head slightly at her. She sank back down next to Bridget.

---

THE LAST REMAINING men and women from Field Hospital # 5 reached Paris a few hours later. They stayed there for a week, recuperating and trying to describe to those in command what had happened as they were preparing to leave the camp. A few soldiers had been sent back to retrieve the rest of the wild men and to see if there were any other victims of their murderous spree. Their bloodied hero had died but just before he had asked that someone save his beloved horse. The army had an obligation to make sure those men were no longer a threat, so they agreed to go back for the horse as well.

Roger had sustained two bullet wounds. The first had caught him in the arm and gone through, luckily for him it was quite easy to treat because it hadn't hit any bones or arteries. The second had left a deep furrow through the side of his scalp, leaving him bleeding badly until they could get him stitched up. Also, he had suffered a hit in the head from a rock that was thrown by the men. As unlikely as it seemed, this wound seemed to be causing the most pain and suffering for Roger. He was dazed, acting very strange, seeming to not understand where he was or how he came to be there.

The doctors that had examined him said it was temporary; they could not see any lasting damage from the wound, but it would take some time to heal, and because of the trauma he could be a little bit confused for a little while. Bridget was understandably upset by this and had postponed going to her relatives. She and Sadie would both be accompanying Roger to a convalescent home back in England that housed and treated shell shock patients. They would be required to stay in the nurses' ward for a few weeks for rest and relaxation and to recover from their own trauma. Then, they would be allowed to work there if they chose. The hospital needed nurses after having so many soldiers and even doctors admitted for mental health problems.

It was miraculous that none of them had been killed by the crazed men. Sadie joked with everyone that she and Bridget were both small targets and so that had probably saved their lives.

They said goodbye to Bertie and Red, who were going to stay in Paris at the Army base for a couple of weeks. They were going to get married and then return to the States. Bridget and Sadie hugged Bertie and there were plenty of tears as the friends all said goodbye. "You girls are like sisters to me," cried Bertie, smiling through her tears. "I want to see you again, and soon."

Sadie wiped her eyes on her sleeve. "Bertie, we will be staying here for a little while. We are being offered a position here, working with the shell-shock fellows, if we would like. I think it sounds good, since I do not know where I'm going just yet. I might as well be useful while I'm making up my mind."

Bridget nodded fiercely. "I'll stay until Roger is well, at least. You and Red must come back and see us before too long, all right?"

Before the couple left, they all had an evening socializing with some of the staff and patients, including other nurses like them. There was much common ground among all of them, and they made many new friends. Roger was quiet; he just sat and stared mostly, no sunny smile in sight, no intelligent conversation or gleam in his eye. He was just…silent. Lost. The doctors said it should not be a permanent condition and was likely due to the injuries he'd taken. Besides that, many soldiers and civilians alike who had been close to the front would suddenly develop the condition known as shell shock. Originally it had been thought that it was directly caused by a concussive blast near the sufferer, but new evidence showed that many of the men were not near any bombs or loud explosions. It was a mystery. Sometimes the men would recover, partially or fully; in other cases, they remained locked inside the strange world of a tortured mind. No one knew exactly what key, if any, would bring them back.

# PART III

## 23

### JUNE 1919

**Paris, France**

Matt lifted one arm up, then down, mimicking the doctor as instructed. Then again, and again, and another five times until the doctor was sure he had the required range of motion to declare him healed. It had been a long journey. His head was finally clearing up and his memory was returning, although not every detail that should have been there was present.

When Matt had gone with the mercenaries to rescue the officer and his men from up near the Chateau-Thierry, things could not have gone better during the actual mission. They had distracted the Germans, gotten the men out, and made their escape with no serious injuries. After riding hard for a day, they decided to stop at a good-sized, deserted farm and stay in the barn for a few days so everyone could rest. The fellows they had rescued had been trapped a good week or so and were malnourished and exhausted.

They all slept in the big barn while four of their number kept watch at night. While they thought that they were safe enough, on their second night there, two of the men on guard had their throats cut. One of the remaining two got off a warning shot before all hell broke loose.

A volley of gunshots went off, and there was a loud bang, and suddenly the barn was on fire. Everyone rushed out only to be met with axes and blades being wielded by crazy men, civilians it looked like. They were filthy and ragged and seemed as if they were barely human. They were bent on death and thievery. Matt feverishly worked to get all the horses out of the barn. As he let the last one out, he was struck on the head from behind and knocked to the ground. Dazed, he tried to get up when someone clubbed him again, knocking him out. He lay unconscious as several men kicked him repeatedly, then grabbed at him to see what, if anything, he had in his pockets. One of them raised his axe to strike Matt dead when a shot rang out, spinning the man around and killing him. Some of Matt's group had managed to kill some of the wild men. The fellow that shot Matt's attacker stooped down to get a look at how badly Matt was injured.

After it was over, about half of the mercenaries were dead, and many were badly injured. The wild men had run off. There had been so many of them there was no way to stop them.

It had taken some time to round up the horses and construct a couple of travois to transport the most seriously wounded. They did not take time to bury the victims because they didn't know if the crazed men would return. They needed to get the injured men to a hospital and soon. They set out the next morning, taking it slow for the sake of those with broken bones. It took them all day to reach a field hospital, and by then several of the men were in terrible shape, Matt included.

One of the vicious kicks he had received had cracked his femur, his collarbone was broken, and he had received an ugly blow to the head that had caused him to lose his memory.

It had taken months for him to heal, and his memory was still not back. He remembered most things, but he had lost most of the time he had been on the front. He saw that he had burn scars on his ankle but could not remember how he had gotten them.

Everything was hazy, and he would get headaches trying to remember. The doctors said he might regain his memory, or he might not. At best he would get most things back; at worst, none of it. He was frustrated on some days because he felt like he should be progressing more than he was.

He wanted nothing more than to return to the United States. His doctor had promised him that after a little more time he would be able to handle the voyage home. It could not come soon enough. He was bone-weary. He was hoping that once he was home, his memory would come back completely. He was forgetting something very important; he was sure.

24

MAY 14, 1919

**Victory Gardens Memorial Hospital - England**

Sadie carefully placed the flowers she had gathered on her walk. She brought them to the patients' rooms, changing them out of the vases where the old flowers had wilted. She put the fresh bouquets in the jars and threw the old bouquets in a bucket. From there, she took the bucket out back and emptied it. Putting fresh flowers in the rooms was one of her duties every day. She enjoyed very much how the flowers brought healing to the men's minds.

Sadie and Bridget had initially come here to assist

with Roger's condition. He had improved so much that the girls were determined to work with as many shell shock victims they could, and as Roger improved, he vowed to take on some patients as well, to work with and help bring them back from that dark and terrible place they had gone to in the mind. They had all committed to staying on until the end of the year. Then, Roger and Bridget would probably get married and go back to America, or possibly go live near her cousins up in Ireland. Sadie would go back to Michigan. Where exactly in Michigan, she did not know.

She had been writing letters to a few friends back home and she sent one off to Maude Beckett, her roommate from nursing school. Maude was staying in D.C. working at a hospital with her new man, and he was a doctor at that. Sadie was excited for Maude; she was a sweet, wonderful girl and was amazing with patients. She had been so much like a sister to Sadie that she felt as if they were family.

But, until the end of 1919, they would be staying on here, helping with the two hundred or so patients. At that point, Sadie felt she would be ready to move on with her own journey. She tried not to think about Matt. Oh, why had he left without even a note? It made no sense. Then she had asked Roger to find out where he was, but Roger had been wounded and had forgotten about it; Sadie was sure that by now he wouldn't be able to track him down any better than she. She would find out if Matt were home in Michigan. If he were there, she could get her answers. If he was not and couldn't be found, then that was an answer also.

About a month later she got a letter from Maude. She was doing well, and wanted Sadie to visit her in D.C. She wrote back that she would stay for a short time, but then had to work out where she was going to live permanently, as she was without a home and family. The next letter from Maude suggested strongly that Sadie stay with Maude's mother, Charlotte, back in Michigan. She had a big house and would love to have Sadie come and stay with her and Maude's father. Maude's father was away on business frequently so Charlotte would love the company.

Sadie was cheered by the letter. The thought that Maude's mother would like her to come and live with her was touching. Sadie had been feeling so alone, and although she had never met Charlotte, the idea of feeling part of a home and family was very appealing. She smiled to herself. She would be in Michigan, and Matt would be nearby, so she would get her answers. Then she could decide whether she wanted to return to Miller Creek or not. She missed her small town and the folks she had grown up with and helped heal for so long. While not exactly family, they were dear to her heart.

Johnny had always been her best friend, and she had been very close to Hilda as a young girl, so she hadn't had a lot of girlfriends. That was why Maude was so special. Sadie was excited about the future for the first time in a long while. Time healed wounds that medicine could not, Hilda used to say.

---

SADIE CAME out of her last patient's room for the day, and saw Bridget walking toward her. As was their habit and schedule, they got finished around the same time so would try to eat together. She looked as if she had lost weight, and Sadie knew nerves over Roger's condition were causing the weight to melt away. "Bridget," she began with a look, "have you been eating?" She walked up next to her and took her by the arm. "Let us go eat supper. I'm starved."

"You know me too well," Bridget said with a grin. "I have been eating, just not as much as I should. I always want to be off checking in on Roger, so I do not linger at mealtime. I guess I'm just worried." The girls went to the nurses dining room and found a quiet spot to sit and eat. They spoke of their patients and the progress some of them were making. Roger was one of the lucky ones; he was responding to treatment and beginning to smile again and look appreciatively at Bridget. Slowly, he was coming back to his old self.

Part of the therapy the men had to participate in was to talk about the war with other soldiers; doing so made it easier to deal with the sights and sounds that were still in their minds. It was common for all the patients to have night sweats, nightmares, and even jump at any loud noise they might hear occasionally. Most of the time the grounds of the hospital were quiet as it really helped with the healing process to keep the environment around them quiet.

As was usually the case, the men's dining room was quiet; mostly subdued conversations took place during mealtimes. After supper, in the early evenings, the men would socialize a bit more, play cards, chess and other games, and slowly, over the course of a few months, most of them were coming back to themselves. As they made peace with the demons of war, they became more like the men they had been before the war. Not completely. That would more than likely never happen. But, functional, happy, restored enough to go home and live a somewhat normal life.

The soldiers that did not do well, some would have to have care for the rest of their lives. There were certain men that had the true shell shock symptoms, shivering, twitching, loss of ability to speak or hear or see. Those poor souls were lost forever.

Sadie had forty patients that she worked with. They were mostly non-verbal and needed complete care. She tried to reach them by talking softly to them and mentioning their families' names to them to try to break through the barrier that kept everyone out. Sadie had good luck with this, and perhaps her manner or her tenacity, something seemed to reach these poor fellows, and before long she was making real progress with them. Once they came back, it seemed to stay with them, they did not regress. She was thrilled to find yet another aspect of healing that she could be helpful with.

She also continued to administer teas and tinctures that were specially made to help with mind troubles, dark moods, melancholy, forgetfulness, and so on. She found many plants and herbs as she took walks both on and off the grounds of the hospital. She found a small room where she was allowed to keep the herbs and tinctures and tins of poultices. Since she was dealing with more spirit and mind issues, she used more teas and tinctures and less poultices. She had several patients who swore they were improving after drinking her herbal remedies. It took several weeks in many cases, but she was happy to feel as if she was contributing to their overall health. There was no cure for the horrors of war, but the men seemed to be improving. It took her mind off Matt, and her own bad memories of the war to help others.

## 25

### SEPTEMBER 7, 1919

Matt was finally home. He had gotten off the ship in New York and then taken the train down to Ft. Custer where he would be finishing out the last year of his service in the Army. He would train horses and riders with the cavalry. Henry, his brother, had written that he wanted to raise, train, and sell horses to the military, and Matt could think of no one better to do that job. Henry offered Matt a job working with him, but Matt thought he might try selling or fixing cars after the Army. So, he was going to finish his year and then get out. One more year and he would have ten years in. That was enough for him. He was not quite right yet but mostly healed. His memory was still spotty after all the time in the convalescent hospital.

Now he was getting finished working with a group of new recruits. They were showing him what they could do as far as riding skills. Some of them reminded him of himself when he had first started out, all blazing eyes and hot-blooded, riding like they were born in the saddle.

When Matt had started out, he was in the National Guard and was only seventeen. It was hard to believe that these boys were a year older than he was when he began. They looked so young to him. He did not have a long time to go anymore and he would have ten years in. It had been a rough year with the war and his long recovery. He was ready to be done with the Army. He wanted to be a civilian and work on the farm and repair cars and tractors. He wanted to live a nice, dull life.

His memory was getting better every day. He felt at this point that it was only a matter of time before it all came back. He brought his horse to the barn and took care of him, then went to wash up and get to the mess hall. He was in the middle of supper when it hit him.

He remembered running through the night and getting blown up, which is where his burns came from, and his ankle sprain. He remembered the field hospital, where a very pretty girl with green eyes and miles of curly dark hair was his nurse. He could almost remember her name. He was encouraged that he would think of it. She was important, he knew it. He paused for a moment. A slight pain formed behind his eyes. The doctors had told him to not try too hard to remember, but to just let it be, and it would come back. He hoped they were right.

## 26

### NOVEMBER 1919

Sadie brushed the last bit of lint off from her beautiful silky gray and green gown. The hospital was having an autumn dance tonight and she was excited to have something pleasant to do. She enjoyed dancing very much and was getting pretty good at it. They had held many dances at the hospital; it gave the patients and staff alike something social to attend, and they all needed it desperate after the long war. Bridget and Roger were to be married at Christmastime.

Sadie had been planning on going home to Michigan to stay with Maude's family, but now she was not sure. She really had enjoyed her time at Victory Gardens and had seen such promise with the men she worked with that she did not want to stop working there yet.

The dining room had been transformed into a ballroom. Autumn colors were abundant, pots of mums and vases of sunflowers were everywhere, and there was a band getting ready to play. Sadie spied Bridget in a lovely bright blue dress trimmed with lace and went to her. Bridget's red hair was so becoming with her dress, and Sadie told her so.

"Thank you, dear! You look so lovely in that gown! I declare, you have the prettiest eyes I have ever seen. My, there are a lot of handsome gentlemen here, don't you agree?" Bridget grinned at Sadie and nudged her gently. "You shouldn't have any trouble having your pick of the men."

Sadie snorted in a very unladylike fashion. "Bridget, you are spouting nonsense. I'm just a little country mouse." Then she laughed at the thought of a mouse in a dress.

"Where is Roger? He is usually stuck to your side?" Sadie glanced around as she spoke. "Oh, there he is."

Roger entered the room with a couple of friends. He was as handsome as ever, winsome smile back in place as he was nearly completely recovered. He was working at the hospital as the girls were, managing different groups of men as they discussed their war experiences and trying to work out ways to cope with their condition. "Shell shock" was a broad term; it covered the physical cases of shaking, twitching, and trembling as well as the mental aspects; cowering at large noises, fearful in crowds and so on. There were many sides of it, and it was a puzzle to all of the doctors. However, most of the men were making vast improvement. Time would tell if it lasted as they made their way home. The soldiers all seemed to react badly to loud noises; that would be one thing that would never go away. They would live with that particular terror for the rest of their lives.

The music began, and Roger and Bridget began to dance, just as a handsome officer extended his hand to Sadie. He was a thin man with dark hair and pleasant features. He had the kind of lines around his eyes that only get there by the hard things in life. Sadie knew he had been a patient here and that he was getting well. She went spinning around the floor with him, having a marvelous time. His name was Captain Bricker, and he was very much a gentleman. After the first two dances, they went off to the side to speak with Bridget and Roger. They were getting a drink and visiting with some other friends.

Sadie saw her friend Monica and went to say hello. Monica, another nurse, was a blonde beauty, slightly chubby but an absolutely shameless flirt. All the men wanted to dance with her whenever they could.

Sadie danced with several different men, wishing she could feel something for them the way she had with Matt. How was it that one man could affect her so? She sighed. Not now. She was going to have a wonderful time tonight. She went whirling around the floor with another officer; he was a big man but light on his feet and it was dizzying how quickly he moved. She was laughing and flushed when they got finished.

"I believe I need a rest," Sadie chuckled. "You are quite a dancer!"

The officer grinned. "You are easy to spin, my dear." He bowed, then excused himself to ask Monica to dance.

Sadie had a fun evening. She was getting ready to say goodnight to everyone as she really was tired when Roger approached her. "You can't leave without dancing with me at least once," he teased.

"Oh, really?" Sadie laughed. "You seem to have had your arms full all night."

Roger smiled at her and they began dancing the waltz. "You are my second favorite girl," he said, enjoying every moment. "You really look lovely, Sadie."

"Thank you, Roger. I am so glad you are doing well. We have all had quite a time of it, haven't we?"

He nodded. "I will miss you and I know Bridget will as well. We seem to have decided to stay near her cousins for a while. It is a quiet little spot and that will be good for both of us. Just for a little while. Then, we will probably settle here. I have relatives that are still near London."

Sadie replied, "You will have to come to America to visit me. I am going to stay with my friend Maude's family for a little while. I just wish that I could forget about Matt. Why can't I enjoy the company of one of these nice men?"

Roger looked at Sadie directly. "If you still feel that way, then you must love him. You cannot stop that. You either get on with your life or you try to find him. But you can't ignore what you meant to each other."

Sadie was thoughtful for a moment. "I think I feel the same about him as I did in France. I don't seem to feel that way about any other man I've met here." She sighed loudly. "I just wish I knew if he was even still alive. I want to see him again so badly."

Roger nodded. "Then I think you've answered your own question." The dance ended and Sadie said good night to everyone. It was getting late.

## 27

### ONE YEAR LATER

While the last few months had flown past, this week was dragging on. Sadie was packed and ready to go home. She had witnessed Bridget and Roger's wedding ceremony and watched them leave to go to Ireland. They had cried when they said goodbye. They had become as close as sisters; watching Bertie and Minnie move on had been hard, with Bridget, it was devastating. Sadie had grown accustomed to loss on some level, and she knew that this loss was different, not permanent, and that she would see them again.

Now it was time for her to move on. She was to board a ship home in one more week. She hoped there would be no rough seas. One could never know for sure about the ocean; it seemed to have a mind all its own and could go from peaceful to angry very quickly.

It was late November 1920, and the war had been officially over for two years.

Sadie had spent the last year working with the patients at Victory Gardens and had even gone out on a date with a few different young men. There had been a few parties, dances, and celebrations to enjoy. She just had not felt anything as special as when she had been with Matt. It seemed like a distant memory. It had been over two years since she had seen him, and they had only had a short time together. She was convinced by now that it had meant nothing to him. She would be fine, after she returned to Michigan. She was excited to see Maude and meet Maude's family.

As it happened, the voyage went well, with only a few squalls and slightly rough seas. Sadie was back in New York on the 18 of December, and Maude met her at the shipyard. The girls embraced and cried. It was so amazing for Sadie to be back on American soil, with her best friend from nursing school. Maude was married now, to her doctor, and Sadie couldn't have been happier for her.

She was going to stay with Maude in D.C. for a couple of weeks, then she was headed back to Michigan. As they got onto the train from New York to

D. C., Maude said, "I can't wait to tell you, I've seen Matt, and he is as good-looking as he ever was. He has a little bit of a limp, but other than that, he is doing all right. Do you know what happened to him?"

Sadie frowned, "What do you mean?"

"Sadie, you won't believe this. You remember the group that attacked you just before you left the field hospital?"

"Of course, I'll never ever forget." Sadie felt uncomfortable thinking about it.

"That same bunch attacked Matt! Oh, my goodness. I have to start at the beginning."

Maude told Sadie how Matt had been called out during the night to ride fast to reach a group of mercenaries that were being hired to rescue an officer and some of his men that were trapped between two lines of Germans.

"They had gotten out safely, but while they were resting up for a few days, that band of outlaws attacked them, killed many of them, and beat Matt up something awful. He had a head injury and he lost some of his memory. He got it all back some months back, but it was a long recovery for him."

Sadie got tears in her eyes. "What on earth? The same group." She would never forget those haunted, dirty faces with their wild, hopeless eyes. A shudder went through her.

"How is he now? Is he all right?" Sadie held her breath.

Maude smiled gently. "He is doing all right. He is finishing up his time in Army. He has been in it for a long time, and he's had enough. He is almost completely back, but the biggest thing is, his memory isn't quite right. He is thin, and he looks a little tired, but you know how it is, with the nightmares, loud noises and such." Maude was quite sure Sadie understood all too well.

Sadie suddenly felt the need to see Matt. She didn't want to wait anymore. But she promised Maude a visit. Maybe she could cut it a little shorter.

Maude seemed to read her mind. "We'll make sure we get you on a train home before too long." She giggled.

---

MATT GATHERED his things together and got ready to board the train from Ft. Custer to Grand Rapids, Michigan. He was officially finished with the Army. It felt good to be a civilian again. He'd been just a kid the last time he was non-military. He was ready to see his family and the farm, and all his friends from back home. It had been a long time.

Henry was staying at the farm for now, with plans

to buy it from their folks. Matt was going to rent a place in town so he could be near where he hoped to work. He wanted to sell cars and repair them and so on. He appreciated a fast car as much as a fast horse. Henry was going to train horses for the Army and Billy Beckett was going to work for him.

Matt had gone home for a brief visit in October. He had wanted to make arrangements for a job before he came home. With so many boys coming home from the war there were not a lot of jobs to go around. He was fortunate that he had found an old friend of the family that was going to hold a job for him. He would be test driving, selling, and repairing cars, which suited him just fine.

His memory of the beautiful nurse haunted him. He couldn't remember anything else other than her beautiful face, her calm demeanor and soothing voice. He could almost remember her name. He saw her suddenly, in his mind's eye, falling. He ran to catch her! His heart skipped a beat. He remembered kissing her, her crying in his arms. Sadie! It was Sadie Prentiss, and he was fairly certain that he loved her!

All the remaining puzzle pieces came to him over the next few days. He needed to write her soon and find out where she went. He had no earthly idea where she was. What had she thought all this time? Did she even remember him? Had he imagined those feelings?

## 28

Just as life seemed as if it would go one way, it went another. Sadie had been at Maude and John's for only a few days when she began to feel ill. She had a fever and was dizzy. Maude put her to bed and stayed home from her job at the hospital to care for her.

Sadie felt as if she couldn't breathe. She told Maude which herbs she used for coughs and fevers and Maude made some teas for her. She sipped them all day long, hoping they would help her breathe easier. Sadie was sick for three weeks, with fever coming and going and such horrible aches she wanted to die. She didn't understand why she got the flu now, after all the times she was exposed to it and never got sick. She wished Hilda were here; that would have made her feel better. Even though she was with Maude, she felt alone and sad.

When she finally began to feel better, John, who was a doctor, told her she was too weak to travel and shouldn't go home for a while yet. She understood, but was frustrated as she was so looking forward to seeing Matt. Maybe he didn't even feel that way for her anymore. She sighed. She was so tired of lying in bed but did not have any energy to get up.

---

MATT RECEIVED a letter from Maude stating that Sadie had the influenza and wasn't able to travel back right now. He felt terrible thinking of his Sadie so sick in bed. She was such a feisty little thing; he couldn't imagine her being down for too long. He had written a letter to her and she hadn't written him back. Maybe it was too late. Perhaps she had met someone else. She would be staying with the Becketts so he would find out soon enough. In the meantime, he had to carry on with his life.

He was settled into his apartment and was working at the car lot. He loved driving the cars and had enough money saved to buy his own shiny new car. He was returning home one evening when he saw an Army friend waiting outside for him. What was this about? He got out of the car and shook hands with his friend, Reggie. "What on earth brings you by here?" Reggie was a buddy from the cavalry and Matt hadn't seen him for two years.

"Brother, I have a problem." They went inside and had a drink. They stood in the kitchen for a moment, then Matt said,

"Let's sit, that's what the new furniture is for." Reggie laughed.

"How much money would it take for you to come down to Texas with me?" asked Reggie somewhat hesitantly.

"Texas? What the hell for?" Matt was a little irate. He had just settled in and had a new job, not to mention Sadie was supposed to come back to Michigan any time now.

"A whole lotta horseflesh. My brother Elmer actually rescued around a hundred horses that were being kept by some Mexican outlaws. They were captured on warrants and this is the good part: My brother, if he chooses, can keep the horses. The horses are in rough shape, some of them, and need some care before they can be moved. Thing is, I am going to go there and help him out, caring for the horses until they are ready to be transported. Then, he said I can have half of them. I don't know anyone that knows more about horses than you do. I wondered if you would come down to Texas with me and help me out. Now, if you can't, I understand, I haven't seen you in a long while and I have no right. No hard feelin's".

Matt sighed. "What are you thinking your timeline is, and how much money are you offering?" Matt was like most young men; he wanted to buy a house and some land, maybe a few horses.

Reggie shrugged, "The timeline is probably around three months, maybe four, depending how bad of shape the horses are in. If he gives me half the horses, I'll give you half of mine. That would be around twenty-five, saying they all make it. Plus, the cash reward that Elmer received from catching the outlaws will pay for expenses while we're there."

Matt was staggered. That was a huge offer, and he knew he couldn't say no. He rubbed his hand over the back of his neck.

"Let me talk to my boss at work." He grinned at Elmer. "I think I'm going to Texas!"

## 29

### JULY 2, 1921

Sadie was thrilled to have some girls to talk with again. She had been missing Bridget something fierce. After recovering from the flu, she had headed off to Michigan on the train. Charlotte had met her in Grand Rapids, and when Sadie met the lovely, black-haired woman with the icy blue eyes, she felt as if she had arrived home. She got on very well with Charlotte, and couldn't wait to meet Ellie, Evelyn, Charlene, and the boys, Billy, Bobby, and Henry. And Matt. She couldn't believe she hadn't seen him in so long. He had told her he was from Michigan, and now she couldn't remember whether he had said he knew Maude. It was just a wonderful coincidence that the fellow she met and fell for was a childhood friend of her nursing school friend.

Ellie and Charlene were so welcoming to her that Sadie felt as if they were sisters. She had quietly told them that she had run into Matt overseas, but she hadn't given them any details. She kept that pain private, not wanting to examine it too closely, certainly not wanting to share it with anyone.

After all this time, it turned out that Matt was out of the Army, but he was currently helping a friend down in Texas. He was returning home and she would finally see him. How would she even recognize him anymore? She couldn't for the life of her remember if Matt had mentioned knowing Maude's family. She and Matt had not had much time together; they hadn't talked too much about their lives back home other than that they were both from Michigan. She wondered for what seemed like the thousandth time if he had mentioned her to his family.

Did she truly remember him? She recalled his handsome face and charismatic smile. Then she remembered some extremely passionate kisses and her face grew warm. She remembered him just fine.

Sadie spent the summer having picnics by the lake with Ellie and Charlene and their families. She was relaxing for the first time in her life. There was no one to wait on, or nurse, or lives to save. Ellie and Billy were absolutely smitten with each other and so were Henry and Charlene. Sadie heard the story about how

Henry always thought he was going to marry Ellie, so she was tickled to see how it had turned out. Life was sure strange sometimes. She couldn't imagine Henry with anyone but Charlene. Henry was different in looks than Matt, but he had a similar smile, and it was a little strange for Sadie to see that smile on a different face.

She wrote to Bridget and the other girls from France, and she heard back that Minnie and Marty were getting married. She was thrilled for them. Now three out of the four of them were happily settling down and Sadie, while happy for them all, felt a little envious. Would she ever find someone? She was happy enough, but still missed her brother greatly, and thought of Matt often enough that it was a distraction. She had been pleased to hear that Minnie and Marty would be settling in Ohio, so the chances of her seeing them again were pretty good. And Bridget had promised to come to visit her, and she was greatly looking forward to that.

She helped the Dawson girls with their garden and then with canning and preserving. Aunt Nettie, as she insisted Sadie call her, was a force to be reckoned with. Sadie, not having a mother of her own, was in awe of all the things Nettie managed between the D.A.R. projects and running the household and organizing events for the lake crowd.

It was a quiet, refreshing time for Sadie. She felt as

content as she ever had. She wanted to go back to nursing, but for now, this was close to heaven. She always had been a hard worker, so she didn't mind one bit helping with all the cooking the Dawsons did. She had a few lingering nightmares from the war, but they weren't too bad anymore. At first, she hadn't slept through the night without waking with a start repeatedly, jumping at every loud noise and sudden sound that she heard.

The D.A.R. ladies were working on a fundraiser to help gather food and clothing for the orphans in France and Belgium. There was to be a dinner and dance in September. Sadie went with Ellie and Charlene to buy a new dress. It had been a couple of years since she had purchased a new dress, and she wanted to look pretty in case Matt actually was there.

Sadie found a deep green silk dress with fringe along the bottom and that had a matching headband with sequins and feathers in matching green and. It was the most outrageous dress she had ever seen; certainly nothing she would have ever chosen before the war. She couldn't wait to wear it. It was so freeing to lose the cumbersome nursing uniforms and even the normal day dresses she used to wear. She was tempted to cut her hair. Many girls were bobbing their hair and she had to admit it looked wonderfully comfortable and cool, especially during the heat of summer.

She had attended plenty of dances in the last two years. Fundraisers for the hospital, parties for the patients and staff alike had given her many opportunities to practice. Now, would she get the chance to dance with the one man she wanted to dance with more than anyone? She barely allowed herself to think of it.

## September 8, 1921

THE NIGHT of the D.A.R. dance was hot and unseasonably warm. What that meant was that every so often there was a hot humid stretch of weather. Sadie was going to go to the dance with the Dawsons. She complemented both Ellie and Charlene on their dresses. They were both stunning with Charlene in red and Ellie in white. Ellie's mouth dropped open when she saw how long Sadie's hair was when it was worn loose.

"My stars, that is more hair than I've ever seen! It's so beautiful! I've never seen it down before." Sadie's hair fell in long dark curls to her waist. The green silk dress and headband brought out her strikingly green eyes and was perfect with her nearly black hair.

Sadie laughingly replied, "I will regret it because it is hot. But I needed something different tonight and short of cutting it, this is the best way to wear this." Her eyes darted up to the headband. "It feels a little silly, but I do like it."

Charlene giggled. "I agree about the silly part, but they are so fun, aren't they! And they are the height of fashion."

Sadie sighed happily. "As far as the hair goes, I am sure we will be 'glowing with radiance' because of the heat."

"You mean sweating!" laughed Charlene.

They went downstairs and got in the car with George and Nettie, who was dressed more appropriately in a long dove gray dress with matching hat. She looked elegant and classy, and while she thought the girls' dresses were eyebrow raising, she didn't say too much.

When they arrived, the Ellie and Charlene took Sadie around to introduce her to some friends they hadn't seen for a while. All three girls were catching the eyes of many of the young men there. Henry soon joined them, and just before dinner, Billy arrived. He was tall and resembled Maude in coloring but was very quiet compared to the bubbly Maude. He seemed to have nothing but eyes for Ellie. When the girls saw Maude and John, they hugged her and insisted they sit with them.

It was a lovely dinner. There were beautiful late summer/autumn flowers on all the tables. There were tall vases around the edges of the room that had sunflowers reaching ten feet tall. It was so warm and comforting that Sadie felt a little bubble of happiness inside. She loved the autumn season so much. Dinner consisted of a huge variety of mouth-watering dishes, including ham, chicken, roast beef, corn, squash, beans, salad, and potatoes. Pies including coconut cream, apple, peach, pumpkin and cherry followed was extra special because none of the girls had been required to prepare it. They were all too excited to eat much, however. They caught up with family stories and how the hospitals were making progress with shell shock victims and amputees. New types of prosthetics were being made all the time, so there was help for the poor souls who had lost limbs. And all of them had experience with friends and family dealing with mental trauma from the war.

As they cleared the tables for the dance, Sadie thought she saw Matt across the room, but it was hard to tell as it was dimly lit, and it was a huge room.

A young man asked her to dance, and just like that she was whirling around the floor. She loved the feeling of floating across the floor. After several dances and dance partners, Sadie went to take a rest on the side of the room near some benches. Ellie and Charlene stopped over to check on her. Suddenly Ellie gestured to someone. Sadie craned her neck to see who it was. Then her heart stopped. It was Matt!

# 30

Matt couldn't believe his eyes. There, the subject of all his dreams and memories had materialized in front of his eyes. His Sadie. He stopped still for a moment, then kept moving forward on legs that felt a little weak.

Ellie said, "Matt, this is Sadie Prentiss. Sadie was a nurse on the front. Sadie, this is Matt Smith. He is Charlenes's fiance's brother.

Sadie said through stiff lips, "I remember you. I believe you were sent to a hospital in the field. Ankle injury and burns?"

Matt nodded, feeling strange and happy at the same time. She remembered him! But in what regard? Just as a patient? His mind whirled. "I thought you seemed familiar. Thank you for looking after me."

Sadie felt warm. "I was just doing my job, sir." She couldn't believe how handsome he was. His hair was grown out to shoulder length, and he had it tied back in a neat queue. He was quite thin and had some lines around his eyes she didn't remember.

Matt said, "Please, call me Matt." His eyes seemed a bit mischievous suddenly. He extended his hand to her and said, "Would you like to dance, Nurse Sadie?"

She took his hand and, in a daze, went to the floor with him. His hand was at her waist, and it felt hot. Her hand was on his shoulder, and it felt so wonderful she felt as if she was in a dream.

"I, erm, you do remember me?" Matt said, gazing down at her, studying her beautiful heart-shaped face and sea green eyes. Those eyes had haunted him.

"Of course, Matt. I couldn't remember, or didn't know, if you had told your family about me. I didn't know what happened to you after you left."

"Sadie," he said in wonder. "I can't believe I found you. When I didn't hear from you, I assumed you didn't want to see me, otherwise you would have answered my note."

"You did leave a note?" All of the unanswered questions dissolved into thin air. "I never got it."

Matt exhaled heavily. "All of this time… I left it under my pillow, just sticking out. I assumed you would be the first one there in the morning. Someone else must have found it, or it got lost."

Sadie shook her head in disbelief. Her heart was beating quite fast. He hadn't left without a word! "It was right in the middle of the flu outbreak. The pillows were being burned and all the sheets and blankets were thrown together in the big pot to be boiled. It probably got thrown out." Frustration and regret rendered them both silent for a moment. Then Matt said, "Let's go outside for a walk."

They left the floor and he guided her through the crowd and out one of the exits. It was a warm night, the air felt close and humid, and thunder was rumbling in the distance. Sadie didn't notice. Matt stopped with her just into the shadows, away from people. The light was dim. She could barely make out his features.

"Sadie, until this very moment, I thought you had gone on with your life, that you didn't care for me, but now, seeing you, looking into your eyes, I think, perhaps…" his voice broke slightly, and Sadie flung herself into his arms and pressed her lips to his. He kissed her with two years of pent-up longing. She had tears running down her face.

"Matt, of course I care for you. I have been half-alive since you left." Sadie brushed her tears away and smiled.

He pulled her down onto his lap on a bench and

held her. It was too much. He sniffed and wiped a tear away. They sat that way for a long time.

Then Sadie said, "We lost so many to the flu. Dr. Carter, many nurses and soldiers. And Roger was hurt from the rogue band of crazy men...they attacked you too!" She remembered Maude telling her.

"Yes. So much has happened. I got hit hard in the head, my leg was broken, I don't remember all of it. I lost my memory for a long time. Bits and pieces, you know, it came back so gradually. But I could always see your face in my mind. I never forgot your face." He hugged her again. "We need to get caught up, but for now, your chaperones will probably be wondering where I've taken you." He smiled, and Sadie felt as if the sun had just come up. A loud clap of thunder boomed, and the rain began pouring down. Laughing, hand-in-hand, they ran for the building.

They sat within sight of the Becketts and Dawsons, so that everything would be proper, but they set themselves apart from everyone and talked for the rest of the night. Holding hands, not taking their eyes off each other, they shared everything that had happened since they had seen each other last.

Sadie's eyes were shining with happiness that Matt was here, before her, like she'd imagined so often. It was even more exciting than she could have believed. His hair was so long, and she liked it. He looked like a cowboy. He told her about the last few months, caring for and training the wild horses in Texas. He hadn't known it was going to be so intensive; the horses were in worse shape than Reggie had been told.

Sadie told Matt about how the same bunch of outlaws had attacked the nurses and doctors as they were packing up the field hospital. Matt was furious that they had attacked the very people that saved so many lives.

"They were the ones who tried to kill us. That's how I lost my memory. The same bunch."

"They were gone, Matt. There was nothing left of their decency and humanity. They were starving, and it made them desperate. I pity them, mostly. We had to shoot them like dogs." She shook her head slightly. "Roger got hit, and it wasn't life-threatening, but he reacted as we've seen so many soldiers; trauma to the mind, shaking, he stopped speaking for a time. It was awful. Roger has always been so pleasant, and talkative. I...well, Bridget and I stayed with him for a long time at the home for shell-shock patients. It was called Victory Gardens. I helped a lot of patients. It felt so good to see them responding, doing better without having to go back to that awful war."

Matt's eyes looked haunted. "I know it's not my business what's gone on in your life since I left, especially since you didn't know I left you a note, but…did you and Roger…"

Sadie laughed, then said, "I'm sorry. No, of course not. Roger and Bridget were married a few months ago!" Matt smiled ruefully.

"You must think I'm rude."

Sadie giggled again. "I have always liked Roger, but never like that. It's only been you."

They gazed at each other with pure, unadulterated joy. They talked about the friends they had both lost, how their journeys had brought them back to each other, and they talked about where the future might lead. Matt said, "I've been selling cars, and fixing them. I love cars. I want to take you for a ride in my car!" He laughed. "You will love it!"

Sadie's eyes lit up. "I know I will. I have only ridden in Army trucks until recently."

"Are you…staying here? Please say yes." Matt's eyes looked almost like the color of whiskey. They certainly changed colors. Sadie was lost for a moment in that color.

"Matt?" She hesitantly asked, "Weren't your eyes sort of green before, or…"

He threw his head back and laughed. "My goodness, Sadie, have you heard a word I've said? My eyes are funny like that; sometimes they look green, sometimes they look more gold. Now, did you hear what I've asked you?"

Sadie shook her head, feeling silly. She couldn't explain how she felt nervous around him when nothing ever truly rattled her.

"I asked if you were planning on staying here? In Michigan, in Grand Rapids?"

Sadie nodded. "I don't think I could go anywhere else now that you're here," she whispered.

They sat there, holding hands, for a long moment. Then, Matt took her by the hand, and they went over to ask Mrs. Beckett if it was all right if Matt brought Sadie home.

The air was somewhat clearer than it had been, the storm had washed away some of the humidity, but it was still very warm. Sadie felt the wind in her hair and laughed with joy. Matt was so amazing to be around. She felt so alive! As he gently kissed her goodnight, he said, "I will be back to see you tomorrow night. I can't let you go again."

Sadie took his face in her hands and pulled his head down for another kiss. "I can't wait," she whispered.

## 31

Ellie and Charlene Dawson were getting married by the lake. Matt was picking Sadie up from the Becketts and driving out. The families were mostly back in Grand Rapids now, but the girls had wanted to get married by the lake as it held their favorite memories.

Matt was living in the city, and Sadie was still living with the Becketts. She had formed a lovely relationship with Charlotte; it was like having a mother for the first time. Hilda had been more mentor and grandmother to Sadie, but Charlotte was so warm and motherly that Sadie felt as if she had a family again.

They arrived at the lake and Sadie went to see how Ellie and Charlene were doing. Matt went to speak to Billy for a moment. When Sadie came back outside, they were talking about the war; Sadie could tell because their faces were sober. She heard that Eric Burns had been their commanding officer when they were briefly in the same unit. He had been pretty gravely injured in the war but was getting better very slowly. It had been a while since they'd seen him, and when he arrived at the wedding with only a slight limp and an eye patch, they were happy to see him and clapped him on the back. He was a ferocious fighting man, and a very decent man as well. They both respected him greatly.

Sadie watched with interest at how the men interacted with each other. It was so strange to think that they had fought and survived together, and now they were exchanging pleasantries at a wedding. She was glad to see that all three of the men seemed to be doing well. She shyly approached the trio, and said, "Congratulations, Billy, I am very happy for you and Ellie." She felt very small next to these three big men. Billy looked down at her and grinned, and when he smiled like that, he was so handsome that Sadie could see how Ellie found him irresistible. Then, Bobby Beckett strode by and winked at her! Sadie felt a little tongue-tied. These Beckett boys were a handful! She smiled as Matt introduced her to Lieutenant Eric Burns. The eyepatch gave him a roguish appearance. "Bobby dated Eric's sister Blanche for a brief time."

Billy said with a smirk, "Bobby dates everyone for a brief time."

Sadie chuckled. Bobby was an outrageous flirt. She hoped he'd find the right girl soon. He was so charming; sunny where Billy was a little darker.

She and Matt danced at the reception on the lawn with the band playing. She had the best night of her life thus far. Matt was tall, tanned, and his golden blond hair shown in the setting sun. He was breathtakingly handsome. They went for a stroll along the lakeshore. Sadie could smell the sweet smell of sassafras and the nutty smell of the pine needles and other leaves in the air. Once again, she thought of Hilda and the wonderful times they'd had together collecting plants. She sighed with happiness. He kissed her and said, "Sadie, I would like to take you on a picnic tomorrow. Can you get away?"

She nodded and said, "Of course. I would love to gather some plants while we're out. There are a lot here, but there are a few that I haven't found yet that I was looking for. Where are we going?"

"Just a special place I found that I would very much like you to see," he smiled down at her, touching a lock of her curly hair that was loose from her braid.

# PART IV

Matt was going to ask Sadie to marry him. He was head over heels in love with her. Seeing her again just made it a hundred times more solid. She had been as happy as he had when they had seen each other. She had taken his breath away in that crazy dress and headband. She had practically flown into his arms.

They drove out to a road Sadie hadn't been down before, a few miles outside of town. There was a white farmhouse with a porch going all the way around it. It had several trees that were freshly planted in the yard, and a cute little spring house in the back. The big barn was cheery and red and had a small corral just behind it. A large yard went several acres back and was had fencing all around it. Inside the fence was a herd of horses.

They stopped just at the edge of the long driveway and Matt went around to open her door. As she got out, he knelt down on one knee and said, "Sadie, I love you and I know we haven't been back together very long, but I spent two of the most miserable years of my life without you and I would be so happy if you would marry me." He pulled a box out of his pocket and opened it. Inside was a perfect, sparkling diamond.

She nearly fainted. "Of all the…yes! I love you too, and I am only now realizing how much. I don't need any more time." She knew with all of her heart that this was right.

He pulled her into his arms, right off from the ground and spun her around. This was like coming home from the war for the first time, for them both.

He gestured toward the horses. "This is what I was doing in Texas, and these are mine. I was paid in horses for my help. I can train them and sell them to the Army or just sell them for a profit. I bought this place, hoping that I could share it with you." He put her back in the car and drove her up to the house. He showed her the house, then barn and then he saddled a couple of horses and they went for a nice ride around the property. Sadie had never been happier. This autumn had been the best one she could ever remember, and this would be a memory she would treasure always. The only way she could have been happier would have been if Hilda, her father, and Johnny were here. She knew they were always going to be with her, and she knew that they would be happy that she was with Matt. That was enough.

## *Nine months later*

It was a lovely, warm spring day. It was the end of May, and Sadie and Matt were about to be married at the lake, during the first weekend of the summer season. Today was Friday and the wedding was Saturday, so everyone was in a flurry of activity. Even though Sadie didn't have family, the lake families were her adopted family, and everyone was pitching in. It wouldn't be a huge affair, but there was food to be prepared, guests that needed accommodations, and tables and chairs to be set up.

The Dawsons were hosting the party, and Matt's brother Henry was going to give Sadie away. She was touched by the gesture; If her own father or brother could not be here, then having Henry by her side was perfect. She had grown so close with everyone that they were as close as if they were truly siblings. The girls were currently in search of vases to put flowers in for the reception. They had found plenty of them, now they only needed to find flowers enough to fill them. It was early in the season for flowers, but they had daffodils, tulips, and many spring wildflowers to choose from.

She had already started a garden at her and Matt's home. Matt had been living there since last October, and Sadie, although still living with the Becketts, spent some time over there helping with the garden and the horses. She had a small shed at their new home with her own apothecary started. She had many types of tinctures and salves and of course lots of dried herbs. She loved the fragrance of the little building with all her healing plants in it. She was so contented to be working with the people here that needed medical help but couldn't always afford or get to a doctor. She had made many new friends and looked forward to making many more as they settled into their new home.

Matt had been working with the beautiful horses he had brought back from Texas. They were all healthy now, and in prime condition. Sadie had a couple of favorites that she loved to ride, and Matt had promised her that they could keep those. She smiled thinking of her little black mare, Alice. Between healing and horses, they could teach their children many things. She couldn't wait until tomorrow.

---

Friday evening the families were all sitting around a fire, enjoying the warmth as the slightly cooler air of evening settled in. The days were warm, but the nights still cool. They were in the middle of a lively debate over whether they thought Ellie or Charlotte would give birth first, as they were both expecting in a few weeks. The conversation was getting loud and more and more ridiculous when Charlotte approached the group around the fire. She had been inside putting the finishing touches on the wedding cake.

"Sadie," she said. "Can you come here a moment?" Sadie got to her feet. Charlotte had a strange look on her face. Sadie's heart dropped like a stone. Something was wrong.

"Ye-yes…" she stammered and, heart racing, hurried after Charlotte.

They entered the house. A man sat at the table. He looked familiar, but she could only see the back of him. She looked at Charlotte questioningly. Then he stood up and turned around.

Green eyes, like her own, looked out from under a

mop of dark hair. He was thinner, older, and had a few scars on his face. He smiled crookedly at her, "Sadie."

Sadie's heart leapt, and then soared. "Johnny?" she whispered.

## **The End**

ALSO BY LORI BUSMAN

**THE COMING SUMMER**

https://bookgoodies.com/a/B08DSTHL2R

AVAILABLE ON AMAZON AND IN KU